Moho Wat

I got on my 1999 Family Trip

Racci Anderson

Amazing Indian Children series:

Moho Wat
Sheepeater Boy
Attempts a Rescue

Kenneth Thomasma

Jack Brouwer
Illustrator

Baker Books
A Division of Baker Book House Co.
Grand Rapids, Michigan 49516

Grandview Publishing Company
Box 2863, Jackson, WY 83001

Copyright © 1994 by Kenneth Thomasma
Published by Baker Books
a division of Baker Book House Company
P.O. Box 6287, Grand Rapids, MI 49516-6287
and Grandview Publishing Company,
Box 2863, Jackson, WY 83001

Fourth printing, October 1998

Printed in the United States of America

Library of Congress Cataloging-in-Publication Data

Thomasma, Kenneth.
    Moho Wat : a Sheepeater boy attemps a rescue / by Ken-
neth Thomasma ; illustrated by Jack Brouwer.
        p.   cm.—(Amazing Indian children series)
    Summary: Nine-year-old Moho Wat, a Sheepeater Shoshoni
boy, attempts an amazing rescue.
    1. Shoshoni Indians—Juvenile fiction. [1. Shoshoni Indi-
ans—Fiction. 2. Indians of North America—Fiction.]
    I. Brouwer, Jack, ill. II. Title. III. Series.
    PZ7.T3696Mo   1994
    [Fic]—dc20   94-4074
 ISBN: 0-8010-8919-2 (Baker Book House)
 ISBN: 0-8010-8919-0 (Baker Book House; pbk.)
 ISBN: 1-880114-14-3 (Grandview Publishing Company)
 ISBN: 1-880114-13-5 (Grandview Publshing Company; pbk.)

For current information about all releases available from
Baker Book House, visit our web site:
http://www.bakerbooks.com/

Special Thanks
to:

The boys and girls of Kelly School, Kelly, Wyoming
for being good listeners and helpers
and for naming each chapter

Laine Thom
Interpretive Ranger
Grand Teton National Park

Bill Antonioli
Butte, Montana
for taking me to the
Sheepeater wicki-ups in Montana

Tom Tankersley
Historian for Yellowstone National Park

David Dominick
Sunlight Basin, Wyoming,
and Denver, Colorado
for his excellent dissertation
on the Sheepeater people

Wyoming State Archives and Historical Department

Contents

Preface

The Sheepeater people were mountain-dwelling Shoshoni Indians and their name comes from the Shoshoni word, Tukudeka, meaning "eaters of mountain sheep." Long before Yellowstone Park became our first national park, these people lived in and around the park. Other Sheepeater sites have been found in southwestern Montana and central Idaho as well as in the Teton, Gros Ventre, and Wind River mountains in Wyoming. I visited several still standing wicki-ups which are over a hundred and fifty years old.

Since the Sheepeaters lived by themselves in high mountain drainages, very little is known about these special people. They avoided the "valley people." Most Sheepeaters never owned rifles or horses. They ate small animals, roots, seeds, and berries. In the spring, summer, and fall, they hunted the deer, elk, and moose that came to the high country to escape the insects and heat of the valleys. In the winter the Sheepeater people hunted the Rocky Mountain Sheep that fed on the forage found on the open windblown mountain slopes. The presence of volcanic obsidian rock in great abundance gave them an inexhaustible supply of glass-like rock for their tools and weapons.

Moho Wat's ([Moehoe Waht] in Shoshoni means "without one hand") story takes place in the late 1700s. He and his family lived within what are now the boundaries of Yellowstone National Park. The Sheepeater people were the only known full-time residents of this special area.

My friend, Laine Thom, whose ancestors are Shoshone, Gosiute, and Paiute, provided invaluable help as I did research for this book. English is a second language for him. An outstanding member of the interpretive ranger staff of the Colter Bay Museum and Visitors' Center in Grand Teton National Park, Laine is also a recognized authority on Shoshoni culture and history. He shares his unique knowledge as he speaks to thousands of people each year. I am indebted to him for his many contributions to the book and especially for the unforgettable day we spent at the sacred medicine wheel at nearly 10,000-foot elevation in the Bighorn Mountains just east of Lovell, Wyoming.

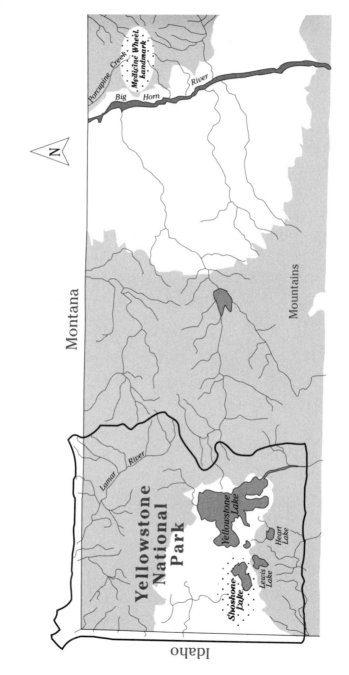

1

Boiling Water's Power

Moho Wat the Sheepeater (Shoshoni Indian) boy was seeing the ninth summer of his life move toward another winter. As he crawled from his family's wicki-up, he headed to the open slopes above a beautiful mountain lake. The aspen trees were a spectacular gold color against the blue sky. The small boy thought about the long winter soon to come to this high mountain land.

Moho Wat had seen many hard days. He remembered nearly starving when hunting was bad. He remembered freezing cold and blinding blizzards that never seemed to end. He would never forget the death of his older brother. It was the saddest day of Moho Wat's life. He loved his brother. He could not understand death. Why did it have to come to his brother? What happened inside Eagle Claw's body to cause him to become stiff and cold?

Eagle Claw, Moho Wat, and their father were skilled hunters. They always used perfect teamwork to bring down deer, elk, moose, and mountain sheep. Silent hand signals between the three hunters helped them outsmart the wary game animals. Now it was only Moho Wat and his father, White Fox. Eagle Claw lived only in Moho Wat's memory.

Yes, Moho Wat had seen many hard days. He also saw good times. He felt proud when he had done something to help his father to bring down an animal with a well-shot arrow. Coming home with meat and hide was a happy moment for a young boy. Someday Moho Wat would find the arrow to drop his first animal. He already had several near misses. Oh, how he wanted to hit his target as he had seen his father and Eagle Claw do so many times.

Like other Sheepeater Shoshoni people, Moho Wat and his family lived far above the valley people. The Sheepeater people wanted to be far from the killing, stealing, and kidnapping that happened in the valleys. Moho Wat's wicki-up was well hidden under giant fir trees in a narrow drainage above a beautiful mountain lake. Someday this lake would be named Shoshoni Lake and be part of America's first national park, Yellowstone. In the late 1700s Sheepeater people lived and roamed all over this land of geysers, hot springs, and boiling mud pots.

Before winter closed in on Moho Wat's family, the young boy's life would change forever. A fast-approaching event would cause a miracle to happen in the lives of the tiny family in this remote place.

Moho Wat's mother, Gray Swan, was busy crushing berries and drying them for winter storage. Along with seeds, roots, and dried meat there would be food for the days when hunting was bad. Every day counted in the race to have enough food to survive the long winter. Gray Swan stood up and handed Moho Wat a hide sack of food as the boy and his father prepared to leave for a hunt.

The boy and his father left the wicki-up with their bows and a good supply of arrows. Black glassy points on the arrows sparkled in the sunlight. Moho Wat's father had taught his son how to flake chips off the black glassy rock using the point of a deer antler. The arrow points were razor sharp and just the right size to be carried by the arrow shaft. Moho Wat loved the hunts. Someday he hoped to shoot as fast and as straight as his father could.

On this day the man and his son walked most of the morning without seeing a single animal. The forest floor was very dry. Each step was measured and each foot directed to a place where it could touch the ground silently. Moho Wat's father always reminded his son "not to step on the sounds." That was White Fox's way of telling his son to walk silently so as not to warn any animals of his presence.

A kill was made that day. Moho Wat's father saw a moose calf nibbling on a willow bush near the lake. The mother moose had abandoned her calf after their second summer together. Moose calves are usually born in the spring. They stay with their mothers for a year and through a second summer. The second fall season the mother moose knows it's time for her calf to be on its own. It is time for her to mate again and give birth to a new calf the next spring.

This young calf did not see or hear White Fox moving closer and closer. The hunter had a big advantage by not being noticed. The closer the hunter could get, the better success he would have with a deadly arrow.

When White Fox saw the calf's ears straighten and turn from side to side, he knew the animal had heard him. It only took seconds for the man to send an arrow to the target. The arrow found its mark. The calf slumped to its front knees. With a grunt the wounded animal raised to a standing position. The second arrow left White Fox's bow. It, too, hit the target. The calf took four steps into the willows where it collapsed and died.

Moho Wat had not seen what took place, but he could hear the calf grunt. He heard the noise in the willows. White Fox called for his son to come. The boy dashed across the meadow and passed close to a boiling hot spring. Many hot springs lined this end of the lake. Moho Wat ran like the wind to reach his father. Suddenly he skidded to a stop, almost falling to the ground. There next to the hot spring he saw a strange sight. A huge sheep head was lying half in and half out of the boiling water. It was the head of a bighorn ram. Only one horn stuck above the surface of the hot water, and that horn made a full curl.

At that instant Moho Wat's father called to him to hurry. Without going any closer to the strange scene, the boy raced on toward the sound of his father's voice.

The moose calf was fat and covered with a prime hide. The meat would be delicious and the hide wonderful for clothing or moccasins. As Moho Wat's father began cutting up the animal, the boy told about the strange scene next to the hot spring. White Fox listened to his excited son as he worked on the large carcass. The busy man didn't get very excited. He just continued his work and thought about how good the hunt had been. The tender calf meat would provide many delicious meals for the coming winter.

Soon Moho Wat was carrying a large load of meat up the narrow drainage toward the family's well-hidden wicki-up. His mother returned with him to the kill site to help lug the precious meat home. White Fox had stayed with the carcass to keep coyotes, wolves, and other scavengers away from the meat. The last trip was made by all three family members. There was still lots of work ahead to prepare the meat for storage.

Moho Wat worked hard and fast to get the work done. He couldn't wait to return to the hot spring for a closer look at the mountain sheep's head. He wondered what the ram had been doing near the hot spring. *Was the whole body in the water? What was the answer to this mystery?* The instant the work was finished Moho Wat took off down through the trees toward the hot spring. He had plenty of practice running in the rugged mountain terrain. The boy jumped fallen trees, avoided tangled roots, and could miss loose rock with inches to spare.

Moho Wat finally broke out of the trees and into the meadow. He was out of breath as he came to a stop next to the ram's head. All that was left of the animal was half of its head. The rest of the huge animal had been eaten away by the boiling water.

The boy wrapped his fingers around the full-curl horn and pulled the remains onto the nearby grass. To his surprise part of the other horn was still there. It had only partially dissolved in the boiling water. Now it was just a long thin strand of horn. It was much too hot to touch.

Moho Wat waited patiently for the long slender strand of horn to cool. When he did pick it up, it fell free of the sheep's skull. The boy held the long thin chunk of horn by one end. He noticed how it snapped back and forth as he raised and lowered his end. The boy could not realize what his amazing discovery would soon mean to him, his family, and all Sheepeater people.

Moho Wat returned to his family carrying the four-foot-long horn. At first his father ignored the boy's discovery. White Fox was too busy making some badly needed arrows. When the man finally looked at his son, he noticed how the long strand bent and flexed in the boy's hand. The father stood up and walked over to his son. The boy handed him the long piece of horn. As White Fox held it and moved it back and forth, his mind raced with excitement. The man had never found a piece of wood with this kind of flex.

"Son, tell me about the sheep's head. Where did you find it? Where is the other horn?"

White Fox asked his son many questions. Father and son returned to the hot spring. There Moho Wat showed his father the exact position the head was in when he found it. White Fox knew boiling water could boil away animal flesh and cause great harm to humans. Now he realized scalding water could even soften a ram's horn.

Back at their wicki-up White Fox spent almost an hour bending and snapping the long strand of horn. He could bend it but not break it. Each time the horn returned to the same shape. White Fox thought how good it would be to have a bow with the bending power of this horn if only it was the right shape.

"Come, my son," said White Fox as he began walking down the drainage toward the hot spring. The boy's father carried the strand of horn with him. His father walked so fast that Moho Wat had to jog to keep up with the fast pace.

At the hot spring White Fox slid the strip of horn halfway into the boiling water. He held it there for a long long time. Moho Wat wondered what his father was trying to do. He knew his father would speak when he had something important to say to his son. Moho Wat had learned to be patient. His father talked very little. When he did speak, his son always tried to listen carefully and learn the wisdom of his father.

As White Fox pulled the horn from the hot water, he reached down with a stick and rubbed it against the hot end of the horn. His eyes were glued to the spot where the stick rubbed against the strand. Finally White Fox dropped to his knees for a closer look.

"Moho Wat, the hot water has softened the horn. We can change its shape. You have made a great discovery. The Above One has shown us a great gift."

White Fox dropped the stick and piece of horn. He walked over to the remainder of the ram's head still lying in the grass. He broke the other horn from the skull and carefully lowered the curl of horn into the boiling water. As he knelt close to the edge of the hot spring, sweat began to pour from the man's head. Hour after hour the man stayed in the same position. White Fox pulled the horn from the water often to check its condition. He became more and more excited each time he pulled the horn from the water. The horn was slowly softening and changing shape.

In the days ahead White Fox and Moho Wat spent hour after hour at the hot spring. They only took time off to hunt. The experiments with the ram's horn would go on most of the winter. When spring arrived, White Fox held the results of his work in his hands. After many tries at molding and shaping, the man had created a beautiful bow from the horn of the mountain ram. Even though not yet perfect, the new bow shot an arrow straighter and with many times the power of any wooden bow ever made. Now the miracle bow could be tried out on a real hunt. Moho Wat was as eager as his father to give the bow its first real test.

2

A Deadly Attack

On a cold damp day that spring White Fox and Moho Wat set out on their first hunt with the new bow. A thick fog covered the Yellowstone Plateau. The two hunters remained close to each other as they approached an open slope. The spring snow was crusted and held them without allowing their feet to break through. This made travel swift and easy.

White Fox stopped at the edge of the clearing and searched the open mountainside for animals.

He silently signaled his son to kneel next to him. Moho Wat's father pointed up the slope at some movement in the dense fog. His keen eyes detected a small flock of sheep grazing on the snowless slope. Wind had blown snow from the open area all winter. Places like these help mountain sheep survive the long hard winters.

White Fox sent Moho Wat up through the trees to a place even with the unsuspecting sheep. The plan was for the boy to continue from there to a spot just above the sheep. Next the boy would leave the trees and send the startled sheep bounding down past White Fox. Hopefully they would pass closely enough for him to have a good shot.

Every hunt took patience and skill. Slowly and silently White Fox moved into a good position. He had practiced for hours with his new bow. Now it was ready for a real test. Would it work as well as the man thought it would? The next few minutes would give the answer.

Moho Wat carried his wooden bow, but his father told him not to shoot. The boy had arrived at his position above the sheep. They had not seen or heard him. Now was the time to walk out into the open and set the plan in motion.

Slowly the boy left the trees. For several minutes the sheep did not see him in the dense fog. Suddenly an old ewe raised her head. Her ears turned toward Moho Wat. Her nose sniffed the air. In an instant she bolted downhill alerting the rest of the flock. The frightened animals burst from their places. In great bounding leaps they tore down the mountain.

Just as White Fox thought, the animals would pass within forty feet of him. The hunter was ready. The arrow was held to the bowstring. At exactly the right instant the man drew the arrow back full length. The angle of the shot was set. Seconds later one of the great animals left the ground on its next leap. It seemed to glide through the air. With split-second timing White Fox let the arrow fly.

The scene was like slow motion. The arrow flew true to the mark. The sheep seemed to somersault in midair. When it slammed into the ground, it rolled head over heels and came to a stop. The wounded animal rose to its feet, took one more weak leap, and fell to earth.

White Fox sprinted to the mortally wounded young ram. He quickly finished the kill. When he looked more closely the hunter could hardly believe his eyes. His first arrow had penetrated the animal's neck so deeply that it came out the other side. The man knew he held in his hand the finest bow an Indian had ever made. Now he could hunt like none had hunted before. He had no way of knowing that this very bow would soon be a lifesaver.

Moho Wat came down through the fog as fast as he could. His father called his name so the boy could follow the sound. Soon the two hunters were together next to the fallen sheep. White Fox was already preparing the animal for the trip to the wicki-up.

"Son, see what the new bow has done. See its power. The arrow sank deeply and comes out here. With the horns of this animal we will make two more bows. One shall be yours."

Moho Wat's heart pounded with excitement. He was eager to get the work done. The boy hurried into the trees and returned with a long pole. Using long strips of hide White Fox tied the sheep's hooves to the pole. Father and son each lifted one end of the pole to his shoulder. The animal dangled upside down between them as they started the long trudge back to their wicki-up.

Moho Wat's mother was happy to hear the news of the hunt. She knew this meant there would be more meat and hides than ever before because of the sheep's horn bow her husband had so cleverly made.

White Fox took time to teach his son how to fashion a bow for himself. The two of them spent many hours at the hot spring melting and shaping the horn from their latest kill. The more they experimented the more they learned. This bow would be even better than the first.

The thick part of the bow where the hunter had his grip was very rough. White Fox knew how to fix it. Along the spine of every animal is a very tough strip of sinew that holds the hide tightly to the backbone.

White Fox stripped this tough sinew from the sheep's spine. He cleaned and dried the strong strand. He melted the sheep's hooves to make a glue. With great skill and care the man glued the strip of sinew to the front of the bow. He rubbed it many times until it was perfectly smooth. When the glue dried, the result was exactly what White Fox wanted. Now his grip felt much better. It would help him hold the bow steadier than ever.

Working on the bow was very exciting for Moho Wat. He felt that he was closer to becoming a man like his father than ever before. He had found the softening horn and now was helping his father fashion the second fantastic bow. Moho Wat had never been happier.

Finally Moho Wat was able to hold his very own sheep's horn bow for the first time. With an arrow to the bowstring he slowly drew it back. It was hard to do the first time. The bow was very strong. His first shot missed the targeted stump by a foot. The arrow slammed into a rock, the point shattered into a thousand pieces, and the arrow shaft snapped in half.

With practice Moho Wat became better and better. He was eager to try his powerful new bow during a real hunt. He had no idea that soon he would leave for a hunt that would threaten his life and change him forever.

Early summer was welcomed by the Sheepeater people. Elk, deer, and moose were leaving the valleys and coming to the high mountain meadows. Mother animals would give birth to their young. They would feed on the sweet new mountain grasses and bushes.

White Fox's family longed for fresh meat. They needed hides to use in making new clothes. Every day the boy and his father left for the hunt. The tragic hunt started like all the others. There was frost on the grass. Birds were singing their nesting songs. Wildflowers were popping out everywhere. Moho Wat felt a chill until he had walked far enough to generate more body heat.

As always, father and son followed a planned course which would give them the best chance to sight game animals. The plan was to move up the drainage above the wicki-up and out onto the open ridges. Each hunter walked up a different side of the gully. This way they could cover more area during the hunt.

Moho Wat hoped this would be the day he would make his first kill ever. His new sheep's horn bow would help. He moved as quietly as possible. Up and up the boy climbed in perfect silence. Up ahead he noticed some bedrock on the ridge. The rock tilted to the right creating a cavelike overhang.

The boy approached the rock carefully. He placed each foot down so as "not to step on any sounds." His silent movement led him closer and closer to the great danger just ahead.

Moho Wat saw the first sign of trouble when he caught a glimpse of a furry ball disappear into the rocks below his feet. Before the boy could react, a huge mother mountain lion sprang from her den. The startled boy barely had time to raise his arms

to protect himself from the airborne cat. Moho Wat
didn't have a chance. In an instant the lion knocked
the boy down and clamped its jaw down on his left
hand and wrist. Down they tumbled off the rocks.
Moho Wat's wind was knocked out of him. He didn't
feel a thing. Things happened so fast, he could do
nothing to save himself from the enraged beast. All
he could do was scream for his father. The big cat
was dragging him off like a rag doll. Soon it would
stop and tear the boy to pieces.

White Fox heard his son's screams. With great
strides the father dashed toward the sounds. He
could see the rock outcropping. He could hear the
screams from the trees nearby. The man sprinted
toward the trees on a downhill angle hoping he
wasn't too late.

The huge cat heard White Fox and plunged on
through the trees. The man's angle was perfect. He
spotted the cat coming into a small clearing. The
lion's jaws were still clamped to the boy's wrist. His
body bounced helplessly next to the great cat.

White Fox knew he might get only one shot. With split-second action the desperate father slipped an arrow to his bowstring. He lunged from his hiding place and dropped to one knee. The surprised cat skidded to a stop. With lightning-like speed White Fox took aim and sent his arrow flying. With a sickening thud the arrow struck the cat in the right shoulder. The angry animal growled fiercely, dropping the boy instantly. The lion pawed at the arrow with its hind paw. As the wounded beast turned to charge the man, White Fox sent a second arrow to its mark. This one glanced off the lion's right leg. It was just enough to cause the cat to veer away and head back to its den.

Moho Wat lay on the ground stunned and in shock. His great terror blocked out all pain. The boy lay still long enough for his father to reach his side. White Fox's eyes filled with the horror of the scene. His son's left hand had been completely torn from his wrist and was hanging loosely by just a few strips of skin. When the boy looked at his dangling hand, he jerked his head to the right in terror. He cried out in fear and pain.

"Lie still, my son," cried his father. "You are bleeding badly. I will help you. The cat is gone. You are still alive."

Quickly White Fox cut the useless hand free. He laid the loose skin back over the severed wrist. The boy's father emptied his hide food sack and wrapped it over the stump of his son's arm. The boy's father told his son to grip his arm near the injury and squeeze it with his right hand as hard as possible. As his father worked on him, Moho Wat's pain began. First it was just a stinging pain, but soon it seemed that his wrist was on fire. The boy clenched his teeth. The pain was almost more than a boy could stand.

White Fox made his son stay flat on his back. After wrapping his son's wrist tightly the father ran into the trees. He rushed back with all the snow he could carry. He quickly packed the snow all around Moho Wat's bandaged wrist. The loose skin covering the wound, the wrapping, the pressure, and the cold provided by the snow would serve to stop the bleeding. Absence of serious infection would be the boy's good fortune in this case. The coldness slowly eased some of the fiery pain. Next White Fox came with water and forced his son to drink. The boy obeyed as tears poured from his eyes.

When the boy was able to speak, he told his father about how he came to the rocks and saw the lion cub scamper into the den. He told how fast the mother lion sprang from the den and onto him.

"Father, there was no time to shoot. My bow is gone. Father, I would have shot. There was no time. I'm sorry."

"Moho Wat, you are a good son. The Above One led you to the ram's horn in the hot spring. Now he has helped you escape death this day. You must get better."

The boy said nothing more. His mind filled with horrible thoughts. *I have lost my hand. Now how will I hunt? Now how will I help my father? Now how will I ever be a man with a family of my own? Will I never have a son to hunt with me?*

Moho Wat was sure his whole life had been ruined. He closed his eyes and fell silent. The boy's loving father hoisted his son to his back. The long painful trip back to the wicki-up began. Moho Wat buried his head in his father's shoulder and neck. The shock caused by the horrible injury began to grow. The boy still could not believe what had happened in just a few short minutes. One minute he was healthy and whole. Minutes later his left hand was gone. *Why me?* he cried inside. *What will my life be like now?*

There was no way Moho Wat could ever imagine what lay ahead. His life had been changed forever on this beautiful spring day. Before his father laid him down inside their cozy wicki-up, the boy's horrendous pain grew worse. This pain would continue for days and days. First his wrist burned like fire. Next came the throbbing that pounded like a thousand hammers. This small Sheepeater Indian boy would live with pain few people have ever experienced.

Moho Wat's mother and father cared for their son every minute. They helped him live through unbelievable pain and suffering. The boy's parents were amazed by their son's courage. They would be even more astonished later when they saw their son prove what he could do with only one hand and a wrist stump.

3

Gift from the Above One

Moho Wat thought the pain would never end. He could sleep only after becoming so tired he could not keep his eyes open. Many days after the attack the boy finally felt the pain ease a little. The skin over the stump was healing. Moho Wat was careful never to bump his wound. When he did, fiery pain shot up his arm.

About a month after the disaster, Moho Wat could rub his stump gently. It felt as hard as a rock. Very little pain was left. It would take a long time for the boy to get used to looking down and seeing no left hand. Often he had the strange feeling that his hand was still there. He even believed he could feel his missing fingers move. He would quickly look down hoping by some miracle his hand had come back. He was bitterly disappointed every time.

Summers are short on the Yellowstone Plateau. Summers always meant visits to places far from home. Many hunters would join in the hunts. There would be meetings with old friends and relatives. There would be a trip to the sacred medicine wheel for worship and gift giving. Moho Wat wondered how others would treat him now when they saw he had only one hand. What would people think? What would they say? The boy started thinking of ways he could hide his stump. If people couldn't see it, he would feel better.

While Moho Wat worried about all these things, his father had something to tell him that would change it all. White Fox called his son to his side. As the father sat working on new arrow points, he told his son a story. Like many stories this one had an important lesson to teach the young boy.

White Fox told about a warrior who had lost an arm at the elbow. Instead of giving up, the one-armed man learned to use his feet, his stump, and even his mouth to do his work. He could even use his feet to hold his bow while he shot an arrow with his good arm. He could lift more than most men with two arms. White Fox finished with these words, which Moho Wat would hold in his heart the rest of his life. "My son, you can still be a man as good as any other man. You can still live a life of goodness and bravery as well as any other man. It is all up to you to do."

As White Fox walked away, Moho Wat sat staring at his stump. His eyes went to his good hand, then down to his feet, and back to his stump. Yes, he decided. He would be as good as any man.

The boy leaped from the rock he was sitting on and dashed into the wicki-up. Next to his bed lay the sheep's horn bow and his arrows. He snatched them up and sprinted to the nearest meadow.

There he lay on his back in the grass. He pulled his knees up toward his head. With his right hand he placed his bow between his bare feet. He placed his feet at opposite ends of the bow. With his right hand he pulled the bowstring back slowly. He felt awkward and shaky. The bow slipped when there was uneven pressure on either foot.

Moho Wat focused his eyes on his toes. Could they work like fingers? He'd try it. With the ends of the bow resting on the balls of his feet under his toes, the boy could control the bow much better. Now he was ready to fix an arrow to the bowstring.

As the boy drew the first arrow back, the arrow slid to the left. It was impossible to hold it steady. The arrow would never fly straight if Moho Wat could not control the arrow on the bow. How could he do it without a second hand? He couldn't think of an answer.

Time after time Moho Wat pulled an arrow back. Each time it slipped but not as badly as the first try. Still, the arrow slipped. Every shot failed. He could shoot but not well enough to hit a target. Instead of giving up, the boy tried again and again to improve.

Suddenly he had an idea. He moved his feet to the center of the bow. Now he could steady the arrow with his big toes. This was the answer. The first shot hit the target dead center. The boy became very excited. All he needed now was practice. The more he shot the better he became. His toes grew stronger and steadier.

From a distance White Fox watched his son shoot. He said nothing. That night at their wicki-up Moho Wat's father said in two days they would leave on their summer trip. Usually the family started their summer journey much sooner. This summer they waited until the boy's arm was healed.

When Moho Wat heard his father's words his heart sank. The time had come. Soon other people would see his stump. He dreaded the idea of being stared at and talked about. He was afraid of the words he would hear. Moho Wat even thought about asking to be left behind. He knew this would be impossible.

The boy walked outside and stood looking at the tall fir trees that hid their wicki-up so well. He remembered hearing stories about the valley people. He heard his mother and father describe the killing, stealing, and kidnapping that happened in the valleys. Moho Wat was happy to live far from all the horrible things that happened far below their mountain hideaway.

The family sat enjoying a meal of roasted deer meat and berries. Moho Wat's mother and father talked about their trip for some time. The boy sat silently hiding his fears and worries about their journey.

White Fox interrupted his son's thoughts. "Son, your father has watched you use your feet to shoot your bow. You do better with each shot. All who see you will know of your skill and strength. They will learn how the Above One led you to the sheep in the hot spring. All people will be amazed to hear about my son and his great discovery."

Moho Wat stared at his precious bow that he now held in his hand. His father's words rang in his mind, "You are better with each shot. Others will see your strength and skill. They will be amazed to hear about my son and his great discovery."

All this gave the boy a warm feeling inside. Maybe he could go where others would see he had only one hand. Maybe he could prove he was still as good as other boys who had two hands. He promised himself to do whatever he could to make his father proud of him. The days ahead would test Moho Wat more than most boys his age had been tested.

The excited boy suddenly took his bow and raced through the dense trees and down the drainage. He broke into the open at top speed. Coming to a stop on a treeless slope, Moho Wat paused to catch his breath. At his feet the grass was all packed down. Like many times before, the boy dropped to the ground and rolled onto his back. Fifty feet away stood the stump of a tree that had been snapped in half by a bolt of lightning. The stump was marred by many direct hits with arrows shot from Moho Wat's bow.

Now the boy's heart beat excitedly. He prepared for his first shot. He pretended many people were watching. His right hand secured the arrow to the bowstring. With all his strength he pulled the arrow back full length. The pressure on his feet and legs was tremendous. The boy held his breath and released the arrow right on target.

Automatically Moho Wat rose to a sitting position. His eyes were wide with excitement. He sprang to his feet and sprinted to the stump. There it was. His arrow had hit the stump dead center. It was driven deep into the wood. Shot after shot Moho Wat practiced. Every arrow hit its mark. Some were so deep he couldn't pull them out. With only three good arrows left he headed back to the wicki-up. Now he was eager to prove himself to others. His father had given him the confidence he needed so badly.

Moho Wat entered the trees and started up to his wicki-up. He had traveled this route so many times he had memorized every rock, root, and fallen tree. He began to think about his sheep's horn bow. He could still see the sheep's head lying next to the hot spring. He remembered pulling the long strand of horn from the boiling water. Yes, it was a great gift from the Above One.

Halfway up the drainage where the trees were the thickest Moho Wat made an abrupt stop. He thought he saw something move behind two giant fir trees in the distance. Like a good hunter the boy froze in his tracks. His eyes searched the trees for more movement. There was none. Still the young hunter stood absolutely motionless.

After several tense minutes, Moho Wat slowly stepped toward the trees. He placed each foot on bare ground to avoid any twigs that could snap and give him away. Any noise now would ruin any chance for a shot.

Suddenly there it was! An animal moved again. Moho Wat could see only a small part of the mule deer's body. The boy's heart began to thump in his

chest. There stood his very first chance for a shot at a live target with his sheep's horn bow.

Moho Wat still was not in a good place for a shot. He had to find a place where he could see between the trees and still lie down for a shot. He had to move a little more. The boy took several deep breaths to calm himself. He made his next moves slowly and carefully. His eyes moved rapidly from the ground to the deer and back many times. As more and more of his target came into view, Moho Wat's throat became dry.

Instantly he came to a stop. The deer's head came up from the bush it was nibbling on. Its large ears turned in every direction. Had the animal detected danger? Moho Wat could not wait to find out. He lowered himself to the ground, fixed the bow to his feet, and drew the arrow back on the bowstring. Taking one final deep breath the young hunter sent the arrow flying through the trees. The arrow struck the deer in a vital spot severing its spinal cord at the base of the neck. The animal dropped in its tracks.

Moho Wat leaped to his feet. He raced through the trees to the fallen animal. He could not believe his eyes. The sheep's horn bow had sent the arrow deep. Death was instant. The boy's mind filled with exciting thoughts.

"I did it! I did it! I made a kill. I made a kill with my feet and one hand."

It all seemed too impossible to believe. Moho Wat was bubbling with joy and excitement. Yes, he could and would be able to do anything a boy with two hands could do.

4

Dangerous Journey

White Fox helped his son carry the deer carcass to their wicki-up. This father was especially proud of his son. He repeated his words to the excited boy.

"My son, you can be as good as any man. Today you became a skilled hunter. Now you know the Above One walks with you."

With fresh deer meat packed and the rest dried and safely stored, Moho Wat's family was ready for their journey. The boy was so excited he could hardly get to sleep. He rolled and tossed on his pine branch mattress. When he did sleep, he dreamed a strange dream. In his dream Moho Wat was surrounded by deer staring at him. When he tried a shot all the deer disappeared into the trees. It seemed he could not keep any animal from seeing him long enough to get off a shot.

The boy woke up often. It seemed that morning would never come. This was the most excited he had ever been about a summer trip. Only a few days before, he had thought about staying home. Now he couldn't wait to be on the move. People might stare at him at first, but he was ready to prove himself to anyone. He was beginning to forget about his missing hand. He even had to stop to think back to the days when he had two hands. This was the only way he could remember how he did things with two hands.

Moho Wat had learned to use his left arm to help lift heavy loads. His left arm seemed to be stronger than ever. His stump had healed completely. It was as hard as the bone that the skin covered. He learned to do many things with his stump that helped his right hand do the rest of the work. His stump could hold down large pieces of obsidian while he chipped away with another point held in his right hand. He could make arrow points as well as he used to with two hands.

Singing birds at first light woke Moho Wat from a deep sleep. He crawled from beneath his sheepskin blanket. Outside the wicki-up the groggy boy stretched his arms and walked to the nearby spring for a drink of the ice-cold water. He filled his cupped right hand and drank quickly. The water was delicious. He then splashed the icy water over his face.

As the boy stood and turned back he saw his mother coming toward him. Gray Swan never spoke much. She talked only when necessary. In her young life she had had two tiny babies die, and only two years before her oldest son, Eagle Claw, had died. Gray Swan's life had been hard. When Moho Wat lost his hand, his mother was there to help him but had little to say. It seemed that she had become numb to all feelings.

The boy and his mother passed each other in silence. Each of them went about their tasks to prepare to leave on the long-awaited trip. Moho Wat saw his father fill his quiver with arrows. Hide sacks filled with food were ready to be tied to each hiker's waist. Hide blankets were folded into a neat square bundle ready to be strapped to Gray Swan's back. She would carry the heaviest load so her husband and son would be free to hunt along the way.

Moho Wat knew he would have plenty of work to do. Each night a wicki-up would have to be constructed to keep out wind and rain. It would be made in less than thirty minutes and be just large enough for the three of them to lie down for a night's rest. Spruce and fir branches were used to make each snug little shelter. The branches were cleverly woven together very tightly and at an angle to shed wind and water. Some stops would be made at old wicki-ups that needed only minor repairs to make them usable again.

Finally all was ready. Moho Wat's father walked ahead, followed by his son and Gray Swan close behind. The small family moved up and up to the highest ridge above their winter home. White Fox would stay on the high ridges to avoid the thick forest and tangle of downed trees. Each afternoon he would descend the ridge and go into the thick trees to find a campsite for the night.

At each campsite Moho Wat and his mother readied a wicki-up. White Fox was off on a hunt for meat. Every day new sights were seen. Moho Wat loved the adventure of exploring new places. The day the family stood on a high ridge and looked down at a great body of water was a thrill for the young boy. The water below was a deep blue, and the lake stretched far to the distant mountains. We now call this spectacular body of water Yellowstone Lake. The Sheepeater people could never imagine that someday highways, hotels, and campgrounds would line the lake and that the water would be dotted with boats.

As Moho Wat stood looking at the great lake on this day, his eye followed the shoreline to the north. He knew his family would head north on the high ridges along the west side of the lake. On the northern end they would cross the river that flows out of the lake and then continue north and east toward the sacred medicine wheel.

Moho Wat remembered earlier trips. The most fun was meeting other Sheepeater people. They always camped together for hunting and for evenings around the campfire. The stories told around the fire were fascinating to hear. Moho Wat especially enjoyed tales about the valley people. It always caused him to wonder about the terrible things that happened in those far-off places. Every story he heard convinced him he would never want to live where there were people who would kill, steal, and kidnap.

Moho Wat's family traveled five days and finally met a group of fourteen other Sheepeater people. There were six adults and eight children from two years old to thirteen. The boy first saw these people from a distance. It was late afternoon. Clouds were moving in over the ridges. A thunderstorm had just hit sending everyone for cover. When it ended everyone got busy setting up wicki-ups for the night. There was no time to visit until shelters were finished. Another storm could hit any time.

As the work was being completed, all the clouds drifted east. The July storm was over, and the sun was about to dip behind the western ridges. A cold chill fell over the forest. A large campfire was kindled. Everyone gathered around to eat and talk. White Fox and Gray Swan knew these people, but Moho Wat had never met these families.

The first person to see Moho Wat's stump was a ten-year-old boy. White Fox saw the young boy staring at his son's handless arm. Moho Wat's father began to speak. The boy would always remember his father's words. He would hear his father tell this story again and again. White Fox always began the story by telling about Moho Wat's discovery of the sheep's head in the boiling water. Next came the tale of the making of the first sheep's horn bow. Then the man described the lion's vicious attack, his shots that saved his son's life, and finally his seeing the boy's hand dangling from his wrist.

White Fox proudly ended his story by telling how his son could now shoot straight and true using his feet, and how the boy had already brought down a mule deer.

As his father told his tale, Moho Wat relived every second of it. The boy felt uneasy and self-conscious at first. During the story everyone's eyes went back and forth from Moho Wat to his father and back again. The boy held his head down and looked at the ground most of the time.

At the end of White Fox's story all of the men asked to see and hold the amazing sheep's horn bows. While they held them, they asked many questions about how the bows were made. Talk went on for hours. The men always asked to see Moho Wat shoot with his feet.

As White Fox's family traveled day after day, they met more and more people. The same story was told again and again. The sheep's horn bows were always the center of attention. Moho Wat's stump was stared at but soon forgotten until people saw his amazing shooting skills. Many boys asked him to teach them to shoot with their feet on the bow. None of them could do it very well. They never wanted to take the time to practice it over and over as Moho Wat had done before he learned to shoot so well.

Twenty-five days after leaving their home lodge, Moho Wat's family camped near a mountain we now call Heart Mountain. Due east a vast mountain range rises to meet the sky. These mountains are called the Bighorns today. Over there at more than nine-thousand-feet elevation and high above timberline lay the sacred medicine wheel.

To avoid most of the danger of meeting the valley people, the Sheepeater people continued north. There they would come to the place where they could cross the open basin the fastest. Soon they would cross a river and climb the lower ridges that would lead into the mountains and up to the sacred wheel. It scared Moho Wat to leave the mountains and enter the valley. He knew there was always a chance of being seen by valley people. He could only hope that they would be good people and not the ones who would kill, steal, and kidnap.

From the first light of day until dark the Sheepeater people planned to finish the crossing of the open valley as quickly as possible. They would stay in trees and bushes whenever they could. Men traveled ahead of the main group to be on the lookout for trouble. In the case of danger they would race back to warn their families.

Moho Wat and his parents joined over thirty other Sheepeater people for the last day of their hurried trip across the basin. The day would be long, hot, and exhausting. The torrid heat sapped the strength of these mountain people. At every stream everyone drank lots of life-giving water.

After over ten hours of walking the weary people finally approached the largest river, now called the Bighorn River. Just beyond this river a ridge led southeast into the great mountains. Moho Wat was eager to reach the river. His throat was dry. His body was covered with dust. His eyes burned and itched.

Moho Wat was near the front of the long line of people when suddenly a runner burst from the trees. He signaled everyone to take cover. Within seconds all the Sheepeater people disappeared into the bushes.

Moho Wat crouched next to his mother in bushes very close to the river. He could even hear water running over the rocks in small rapids. It seemed he had been in the bushes for a long time. Suddenly he heard a new sound. The boy was startled to see a warrior on a huge horse come over the river bank and ride directly toward him and his mother. Seconds later another horse and rider appeared, and another, and another. Seven riders passed within twenty feet of the terrified boy. He could see the powerful muscles of these large men. Every one of them was bigger than Moho Wat's father. The boy held his breath while the riders passed so dangerously close. None of them detected the well-hidden Sheepeater people.

Even after the riders disappeared around a bend in the river far downstream, the people remained

hidden. The sun was getting very low in the west. Moho Wat was so hot and thirsty he could hardly swallow. His skin itched and felt like it would crack.

Finally the signal was passed to leave the hiding places. In no time Moho Wat was over the river bank and into the water. He dipped his whole body under and let the cool water run over him. He came up and began to drink the delicious water. Never in his life had water tasted better.

The boy was just finishing his drink when the signal to cross the river was given. There was still the danger of being seen here in the open.

The people quickly crossed the river in a shallow section above the rapids. From the river bank the men led the way up a dry creek bed toward the long ridge ahead. The rocky gully partially hid the people from view. Spring runoffs had created this gouged-out channel in the rock.

Darkness was closing in as the people reached the tree-covered ridge at the base of the Bighorn Mountains. Like everyone else Moho Wat was completely exhausted. The weather was clear. No shelters would be needed. The trees would provide all the protection needed. It would take the next two days to make the climb to the medicine wheel.

Moho Wat rolled up in his hide blanket and thought about all that had happened that day. Then he thought about the climb ahead. The boy had been to the sacred place four times before. He remembered the last trip to the wheel, which was just before the death of his brother. During that visit White Fox talked with another family about obtaining a wife for Eagle Claw. When a young man was old enough to start his own family all the arrangements were made by the parents of the boy and girl. Eagle Claw's parents would give the girl's family gifts to complete the agreement. When the young people were ready to begin their life together the girl would be given to Eagle Claw to be his wife. Sadly, Eagle Claw died before the day of his marriage came.

Moho Wat wondered if any girl's parents would ever agree to give their daughter in marriage to him. Would the loss of his hand make him unwanted by any girl and her parents? The boy could only wonder. He didn't have to worry about it for several years. He was still too young to be ready for marriage. The weary boy finally fell into a deep sleep.

5

A Big Decision

The final day of the climb to the sacred wheel began in a thick fog. No one spoke. Everyone walked in a line single file up through the cool damp air. Moho Wat remembered the last time he came to the medicine wheel. He walked this very trail behind his brother, Eagle Claw. After his brother's death, Moho Wat's family stayed home for an entire year. They traveled nowhere. They saw no other people. It was a time of great sadness.

When Eagle Claw died, Gray Swan cried out her sorrow to the Above One. She went off to be alone in her sorrow. Believing that her soul dwelled in her hair, she cut every hair from her head and threw it to the ground. With a knife she slashed her arms. All this was done to show the Above One the love she had for her children. When the Above One saw Gray Swan's love for her dead son, he would show her mercy and not let another of her children die. This was Gray Swan's hope. Moho Wat realized how much his mother loved him. He had witnessed her great sadness at the death of her son.

The higher the Sheepeater people climbed this morning the brighter the air became. After one hour the first people in line came out of the fog into bright sunlight. Soon all the people stopped and looked into the valley. It looked like the great cloud bank had been poured into the valley. The view was spectacular.

Moho Wat looked down at the cloud-filled valley. The warm sun felt good. The most exciting thing he saw was a second line of people that appeared out of the fog on another trail a short distance away. Before long four other lines of people appeared out of the fog into the sunlight. The boy wondered how all these Sheepeater people had reached the sacred place on the very same day. When he was younger he never thought about such things. Now that he was getting older his eyes were seeing things differently. He would have to save his questions for later.

The long climb went on and on. Soon there were hardly any trees, only open slopes. Moho Wat could see even more people climbing a trail on the north side of the mountain. Before the day ended nearly one hundred and fifty people would be gathered on the great mountaintop. Everyone still walked in absolute silence. They angled back and forth to cut down on the steepness of their route to the top. Moho Wat's group was the first to reach the sacred wheel. Everyone came to a stop. The sun was bright, and a breeze rustled the grass.

As the sun reached its highest point, one hundred forty-eight Sheepeater people stood silently in a wide circle around the outside of the wheel. Moho Wat saw the elders slowly move along long spoke-like lines of large rock that led to the center or hub

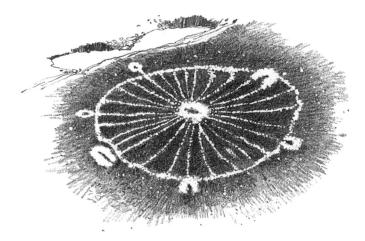

of the wheel. The elders stopped at the hub made
of huge rocks. Next all the Sheepeater people lined
up on the twenty-eight spokes.

When everyone was in place each of the elders
offered a prayer to the Above One. Each man gave
thanks for the sun, for the rain, for the trees, for the
animals, for the grass, for every good thing given to
the Sheepeater people.

Moho Wat's eyes and ears took it all in. All year
long he had lived closed in by mountains, narrow
drainages, and tall trees. Now here he stood on an
open mountaintop where he could see over one

hundred miles in every direction. The boy felt no fear of the open place. He had learned that no people would ever think of doing any bad thing near this sacred place.

For three days the Sheepeater people worshiped together at the great wheel. Even today we do not know who rolled the tons of rock into place to form this great wheel or exactly why it was built. We do know that the Sheepeater people and other Indian peoples used the wheel for worship for hundreds of years and still go there to worship today. Everyone would leave a small gift of thanksgiving, such as a piece of fur, an obsidian scraper or point, a bear claw, or some other item of value, at the wheel. They knew the Above One was watching and listening. During each of the three days no one ate while the sun lit the earth. As darkness came the people moved a short distance away to share food with each other and listen to stories. No one slept very much. There was too much to be enjoyed with each other.

On the second day Moho Wat followed his parents to their place on the wheel. Suddenly a strange feeling came over him. Walking right next to the boy was a girl about his age. For some reason Moho Wat could not take his eyes away from her. She seemed to walk so gracefully. Her long black hair reflected the sun, causing her hair to glow. The ends of her hair moved over her shoulders in a beautiful way. When the boy came to a stop, the girl was only a few feet behind him. Moho Wat glanced over his right shoulder and saw the girl's face. Her eyes were the most beautiful the boy had ever seen. Her face was small and round. When she looked at him, Moho Wat blushed and turned his head.

The boy tingled with excitement. He had never felt like this before in his life. He had seen many girls, but nothing like this had ever happened to him. Several more times Moho Wat turned to sneak a look at the girl and her graceful beauty. Each time he became even more excited.

Time seemed to fly. Moho Wat didn't hear much that was said that day. His attention had been completely captured by the beauty he had suddenly discovered. A strange thought entered his mind. *Would someone this beautiful ever want to share her life with him? Would her parents ever think a one-handed boy would be good enough for their daughter?* Moho Wat tried his best to stop thinking such strange thoughts. He knew it would be years before he would be ready to go off on his own and have a family. He tried to put these thoughts away but couldn't.

During the rest of the time at the sacred wheel Moho Wat could think of little else except the beauty of this girl. He kept finding excuses to go near her. He did his best to hide his stares. When he heard the girl speak to her mother, her voice seemed like a song. Moho Wat was experiencing something people now call puppy love.

Moho Wat said nothing about his feelings to anyone. Soon everyone would leave, and the boy might forget about the girl named Wind Flower. Still the boy wondered about the girl. *Where was her home wicki-up? Was it near Moho Wat's? Was there a chance he would ever see her again?* He knew he might never learn the answers to these questions. How could he know that every answer would come sooner than he could ever dream was possible?

Before dawn of the day to leave for the trip home, Moho Wat and all the people were on the move. It was the custom for everyone to be gone before the sun touched the medicine wheel again. When the boy and his parents neared the river, they stopped for the night. The next morning they headed straight to the shallows for the crossing. No enemy warriors were in sight. At this wide place the people walked into the cool water and waded slowly over the slippery rocks on the riverbed.

The sun's rays had just touched the opposite bank as Moho Wat followed his father up the loose rock. The boy stood on the bank for a few seconds to look back at the great mountain. He remembered the day he had first seen Wind Flower standing near him. He remembered how her hair glowed in the sunlight. He could still see her graceful steps and how her deerskin dress flowed as she moved.

Suddenly, as though a lightning bolt had hit him, Moho Wat was startled by a blood-chilling scream. The piercing sound went through the boy like an electric shock. More screams and yelling followed.

In an instant White Fox went dashing through the willow bushes and cottonwood trees. Moho Wat was close behind. At the edge of the trees White Fox motioned for everyone to keep down. The boy dropped to his knees. He crawled to the edge of a thick clump of willow bushes. The screaming had stopped. Moho Wat parted the bushes slowly for a look. One horse stood in the open space. The rider was standing next to the animal on the far side. He seemed to be struggling to hold something.

Seconds later Moho Wat gasped. The sight was more horrible than he could ever imagine. The warrior threw a person onto his horse stomach down. There she was. Her face was covered with terror. It was Wind Flower. Her small body was pinned to the horse's back by the powerful warrior's hand. Her mouth was bleeding. The warrior had struck her when she screamed.

Moho Wat was tempted to run out to try to free her. White Fox had moved to his son's side and held the boy back. In seconds the warrior was on his jittery horse and riding away. The boy's heart hammered in his chest. His body began to shake and sweat. His father kept signaling for silence. White Fox knew this attack was planned. For some reason it seemed the warrior wanted only one girl, but there could be more trouble coming.

White Fox and a second man finally went to find a safe route away from this place. Moho Wat sat alone. He still could not believe what had happened. Wind Flower, the beautiful one, the one so small and graceful, was captured. *This could not be. Why doesn't someone do something? Is everyone going to let the enemy get away with this terrible thing?*

These thoughts and many more poured through Moho Wat's mind. He wanted answers. He began kicking his heels into the dirt. The Sheepeater people were giving up. They were going to let the warrior have Wind Flower. This can't happen.

The boy's head dropped. He had to decide what to do. Should he give up, too? What could a boy do against such a powerful warrior? Moho Wat stared at his stump. What could one boy with only one hand do against such a vicious enemy? Moho Wat's eyes looked past his handless wrist and fixed on his sheep's horn bow. His head snapped up. He looked all around. Back his eyes went to his bow. A bizarre and dangerous idea flooded his mind. How would he ever dare to think such a thought? His sudden decision could result in his capture or even his death.

I'll do it! I'll do it! the boy shouted silently in his mind. *I'll save Wind Flower from the enemy myself. The Above One has been with me. He will help me rescue Wind Flower.*

Out of sight of everyone Moho Wat moved through the dense willows. In only a few minutes he had left the Sheepeater people still in their hiding places. He was moving north, the same direction the enemy had gone with Wind Flower. The bushes slowed the boy down. Not far ahead he came to a small creek flowing to the river from the west. He turned up the creek toward an open bluff carved out by the river hundreds of years before.

As Moho Wat neared the bluff, he passed a set of horse tracks. In the mud next to the stream he spotted a perfect set of hoofprints. The left hind hoof had been cracked. The boy memorized that print. If he ever saw this hoofprint again, he would know he was on the right trail even if other horses had joined the one carrying Wild Flower.

Moho Wat came out on top of the rocky bluff. He raced to a giant tree uprooted by a great windstorm. Hiding in the upheaved tangle of roots, the boy could scan the river and all the land around it. To the north he saw dust rising from a treeless runway near the river. It was impossible to see anything in all the dust.

Just before Moho Wat started to head north again, he took another look. Wind suddenly blew the dust away. A lone horse stood on the open track. The rider sat upright. Moho Wat could barely make out a second person lying in front of the rider

across the horse's back. That had to be Wind
Flower.

Moho Wat did not move a muscle. He stared at
the rider. He didn't want to lose sight of the enemy.
The boy studied the horse's position on the open
runway. He knew he could go to that exact spot and
pick up the horse's trail if he had to.

Minutes later the rider galloped up a small hill
and disappeared over the other side. Moho Wat
took off on the run. He had to angle northwest to
stay out of sight of the hillside where he had seen
the rider last. Like stalking an animal during a hunt,
the boy knew if he was seen he would fail. In fact,
he might even lose his life if these warriors caught
him. The odds seemed overwhelming against this
one-handed boy. How could he ever save the girl
from such a mighty enemy? He didn't know the
answers, but he knew he had to try.

6

Test of Survival

The only thing Moho Wat had on his mind was to keep on the right trail. There was a chance that he might lose track of the girl and her captor. At the same time, he could not become careless and be seen. He dashed from place to place using bushes, trees, and rocks to hide himself.

Carefully Moho Wat approached the hill he had seen the rider cross a few minutes before. He crouched low as he scrambled along to a hiding place behind a huge dead tree that lay across the rocks at the edge of the hill. From the tangle of upheaved roots Moho Wat was able to observe the valley below without being seen.

The sight below his hiding place sent a chill through the boy. There not far away he saw at least forty warriors milling around a small grassy meadow. Near the center of all the activity five warriors stood on the ground while holding their horses' reins. Moho Wat strained his eyes to see the rider who had ridden off with Wind Flower. He scanned the scene four times, moving his eyes slowly from rider to rider. As his eyes made their fourth trip across the crowded scene, he suddenly zeroed in on one warrior. This rider was headed straight toward the five men standing in a small group in the center of all the activity.

The rider had his back to Moho Wat. He seemed to be sitting differently on his horse. The warrior stopped near the five men and slid off his horse. There she was! Wind Flower was still lying across the horse's back. The boy watched the warrior grab the girl and drag her to the ground. He stood hold-

ing Wind Flower by the upper arm as he talked to
the five warriors.

Moho Wat had forgotten all about time and
where he was. He couldn't take his eyes off the girl
and her captor. He could see them well while he
remained out of their view. Without warning Moho
Wat heard sounds. He had to strain to hear them at
first, but in only seconds they became much louder.
Now loudly and clearly the boy heard horses coming. Moho Wat whipped around to look. Instantly he
knew he was in great danger. Seven more warriors
had ridden out of the trees and were headed right
for him. It looked like these riders had spotted him
from behind.

Moho Wat quickly glanced around for a way to
escape. If he ran downhill, the forty warriors would
see him. If he ran any other direction, the seven
approaching riders would see him. There was no
way out. He was trapped.

The boy shook with fear. His mind raced to find a
way out of this terrible situation. *Where can I hide?*

I have to do something! the horrified boy shrieked to himself.

Moho Wat stood staring at his only chance to avoid capture. When the great tree had come crashing down, the vast root system had torn a deep hole in the rocky surface. Some of the rocks were still wedged in the root system. In one desperate leap the boy jumped into this rocky hole. The rocks skinned his knees and cut his hand and stump when he landed. He had come smashing down at the deepest part of the narrow hole. Moho Wat felt no pain. He was in utter shock. Fear and horror gripped his mind.

The boy could see nothing but sky from his place at the bottom of this six-foot-deep hideout. Horses' hooves hitting the rocky hillside became louder and louder. They were coming closer by the second.

Do they know I'm here? Have they already seen me? If they haven't seen me, how close will they come to my hole? What will they do to me if they capture me? What should I say if they do? The more

the boy asked himself these questions, the more scared he became.

The time seemed to drag. Now the sounds were louder than ever. Moho Wat hugged the side of the hole that was closest to the riders. It was the best way to stay hidden from the view of the passing riders. On the other side he would be seen easily.

The horses' hooves were so loud that they must be at the edge of the hole. Moho Wat hardly dared to look. Then loose rock tumbled down into the hole. Moho Wat hugged the rocks even closer. He slowly turned his head for a look. His eyes were glued to the edge of his refuge. The first rider came so close the boy could see his leg against the horse's side.

The terror-stricken boy held himself stiff. He didn't move a muscle or even dare to breathe. Why did he get himself into such a horrible position? He had moved too fast. He had not given himself an escape route. If these men caught him, he knew it would be his own fault.

Moho Wat carefully counted the riders as they passed. One, two, three, each rider rode on without stopping. The cowering boy could catch only small glimpses of the horses and the riders' legs. Rider number six rode by. One more rider and I'm safe, thought the boy.

There he was, rider number seven. He was almost past when suddenly he reined his horse to a stop. His horse turned. Its rear hooves knocked rocks and dirt down onto Moho Wat. The rider held the horse in place. The animal's tail actually hung over the edge of the hole.

Suddenly the air was filled with the call of the coyote. The warrior above was signaling to someone below him. Moho Wat knew he still had a chance. He had no idea what would happen next. All he could do was wait.

Two minutes later the rider above rode away. He had turned to follow after his six friends. Moho Wat finally took a deep breath. He was shaking. He had come close to ruining everything. He glanced around his hole. Soon he felt a burning pain from his skinned-up body. He blew on his hand and stump to ease the fiery pain. Dust and dirt covered his scratches. He longed for cool water to ease his pain.

Moho Wat's mind started working on his dangerous predicament. *Where are the seven riders now? Are more coming? Whom was the last rider signaling? Are they coming my way?* The boy needed answers fast.

Slowly Moho Wat inched his way up the side of his hole. As his head came above the edge inch by inch, he was able to see more and more terrain.

The seven riders were far down the hillside on their way to the others. The boy could see no one else in any direction. But whom had the warrior signaled?

The boy did not dare come out until he was sure he wouldn't be seen. He strained to see any sign of life in the valley behind him. Finally, he picked up some movement in the trees toward the river in the distance. As he concentrated on that spot, he could hardly believe his eyes. A long procession of women and children was emerging from the trees. They just kept coming and coming. Many women led horses. Each horse pulled two long poles strapped to its sides. The poles were loaded with baggage and food. These travois carried the hundreds of pounds of everything the people needed to set up their village.

Moho Wat was looking at more than sixty families of valley people. They gathered together each summer to hunt and camp with each other. Summer was a time of plenty. There was always fresh meat, lots of roots, berries, seeds, and nuts to eat. The boy had never seen so many people in one place at one time.

It took almost two hours for all the women and children to reach the meadow where the warriors waited. They passed over the hill far from Moho Wat. He kept a sharp lookout in all other directions for trouble. He was still in a very dangerous place. Any minute another rider could come his way.

When all the valley people reached the meadow, only a few minutes were spent organizing everyone. Moho Wat realized that while the women and children carried the belongings, the men had been hunting or out looking for their enemies. Somehow they had seen Wind Flower and wanted her for a prisoner. She had been in the wrong place at the wrong time.

The anxious boy watched as all the people began leaving the meadow heading north through the cottonwood trees near the river. It took another thirty minutes to empty the meadow. Now what would the shaken boy do? He had to get out of his hole. He had to find a safe way to follow these people. They would have to stop long before dark to set up their camp. The boy needed to plan his next move without delay.

Suddenly Moho Wat felt so alone. *Where were his mother and father? Would they think he was captured or dead? Could they somehow know what he was trying to do?* The boy could now only hope for the best. He would keep going somehow.

After looking at every foot of his surroundings by many full-circle sweeps of the area, Moho Wat made a run for a stand of trees just west of him. Safely in the trees he paused to catch his breath. He was sure he had made the trees without being seen, but he would not take any chances. He didn't dare stay in one place too long. Cautiously the boy moved on through the trees. He had his eye on the tree-covered mountainside less than a half-mile away. His biggest problem would be the open space several hundred yards across where he would be out in the open.

At the edge of the open span, Moho Wat rested. He caught his breath, looked in every direction, and darted out in a crouched position. Bent over as far as possible the boy raced through the grass and sagebrush. He stumbled several times but caught himself with his low-hanging arms. He never stopped until he reached the safety of the trees.

Once in the trees Moho Wat set a course due north. He knew if he watched the sun it would tell him how much daylight was left. He would have to make a guess about where the valley people would have to stop to get ready for darkness. He would have to guess when to turn east to find the enemy village.

Nothing stopped Moho Wat's progress until he spooked a white-tailed deer. There was no chance for a shot. The deer had seen the boy first. It was long gone in seconds. Moho Wat stopped for a short rest. He would be alert for any other deer that might be with the one that had bounded away. As the boy stood there, for the first time he thought about his situation. Darkness would come for him, too. All he had was one sheepskin blanket, dried meat, some berries, and his sheep's horn bow and eight arrows. He knew he would have to survive with what he had and anything he could find to help him live from day to day.

Moho Wat's next stop and long look at the sun convinced him it was time to turn east. Somewhere between him and the river he hoped to find the enemy village. His eyes scoured every tree, bush, and opening ahead. His ears were tuned to pick up any sound that could mean danger. The last thing he wanted to do was walk into a trap. He knew now that each step east brought him closer and closer to the enemy somewhere just ahead. There would be no hole to jump into this time.

7

Stalking the Enemy

The farther Moho Wat traveled the more careful he became. He walked silently through a stand of aspen trees. He circled several small meadows where he could be seen easily. The boy was becoming very tense and taut. The least little sound stopped him in his tracks. A startled jackrabbit bounded across his path causing Moho Wat to jump behind a large cottonwood tree. With his heart pounding in his throat, the boy gripped the rough bark of this old giant cottonwood. The bark was a sign telling him the river was near. Trees this size always grew near water.

From high on the sides of the sacred mountain Moho Wat had looked at the winding river below. He could see the river in its present channel. He could also make out places where the river had changed over the years. He remembered seeing the cotton-woods all along the wide river bottom. Yes, this large tree told him he was getting close to his goal.

Moho Wat hadn't walked even one hundred feet from the great tree before he heard a horse whinny. The boy slithered into the thick bushes. He waited for more sounds. The first sound came so unex-pectedly he couldn't tell its exact direction. No more sounds came. Moho Wat couldn't wait for-ever. Slowly he moved from his bush. Now each step was slower than ever. He began to count each step. At number fourteen he saw something move in a clearing straight ahead. All he could tell was that it was something large and brown.

At the edge of the clearing Moho Wat peered between the branches of small aspen trees at an open space. There in a clearing sloping down to more cottonwood trees a large herd of horses grazed peacefully on the thick sweet grasses. He knew he had found the enemy. He had turned east at just the right time. These were the valley peoples' horses, but where was their village? Was it north or south of the horse herd? The only thing the boy was sure of was that he was very close to the village, no matter which way it was.

As before, Moho Wat had to make a decision alone. He had to locate the village without being seen, but how? He would definitely take his time and come up with a good plan. He had already made one bad mistake and ended up hiding in a rocky hole with the enemy riding within ten feet of him.

Moho Wat took his time planning his next move. Just as he decided to circle the meadow, he had a lucky break. He spotted a boy about his same age come out of the trees at the north end of the clearing. The enemy boy walked along the lower edge of the herd of horses. He was obviously responsible

for making sure the horses were safe and not stray-
ing too far away. Moho Wat's eyes followed the
boy's every movement every second. He hoped the
boy would not come up his way. If he did, Moho
Wat would have to drop back into the trees and
bushes to keep from being discovered.

When the enemy boy reached the south end of
the open slope, he turned and headed back. Soon
he disappeared into the trees going north. Moho
Wat was quite sure the enemy village must be in
that direction. Now he was ready to make his next
move.

From Moho Wat's position at the top of the gentle slope, he could look over the treetops and see a
steep ridge rise into the distance. At the top of that
steep ridge he should be able to look right down at
the village if it was where he thought it was. Heading for the ridge seemed like the thing to do.

Moho Wat started a large circle south and east
around the horses. In a very short time he could
hear running water. The river was just ahead
through some cottonwoods and willows. At the

river's edge the boy was happy to see the river curve west a little north of where he stood. That meant he couldn't be seen crossing the river by people in the village. Looking south Moho Wat was sure the village wasn't that way. The riverbank was too steep and uneven down that way.

After making sure he wasn't being watched, the boy skidded down the riverbank, walked across some large rocks, and slid into the water. His side of the river was deep and slow moving. His scrapes and scratches stung when the cold water touched them. He rubbed his cuts softly to clean them out. Gradually the pain stopped. The water felt good, but there was no time to waste. Someone could come by any second.

Moho Wat headed straight for a huge dead snag. The large tree had fallen halfway across the river. Its roots were still clinging to the far bank. Behind the snag lay a pile of driftwood nine feet high. The newly refreshed boy climbed up into the driftwood through a natural opening. Here he rested safely and took time to eat a few strips of dried meat and a handful of berries. He had been going all day on nervous energy without eating or drinking.

Moho Wat was just taking his last bite of meat when he was suddenly stunned to see someone walk out on the bank across from him. There stood a small child with another coming up from behind. The boy and girl each carried a skin sack which they were soon dipping into the water. As their sacks filled, the little boy began splashing the girl. She splashed him back with even more water than he had sprayed on her. They laughed and shouted as the splashing became even more furious.

Moho Wat was hypnotized by this scene. He even daydreamed about the time he had a water fight with his brother, Eagle Claw. They were young then and had been sent to the lake for water on a very hot day. That water fight was lots of fun. Now Eagle Claw was gone to the spirit world, and Moho Wat sat hiding from two children who would surely run for help if they knew he was there. *How fast my life has changed*, Moho Wat thought.

The boy sat motionless while the two children enjoyed their play. When they finally left, Moho Wat slowly climbed through the driftwood and over to the steep ridge. He had to cling to roots to help him up over an overhang. When he reached the trees, he hurried north along the hillside and angled to the ridge top. In less than five minutes he was staring down at the enemy village. Directly across the river teepees covered a meadow. People were busy setting up camp, cooking meals, and talking with each other. Immediately Moho Wat's eyes searched for a glimpse of Wind Flower. He could see her nowhere in the village. What could have happened to her? Had she been taken farther on to another village? The boy felt hollow inside. Maybe he had already failed.

Moho Wat was completely hidden under the branches of a large fir tree. He could stay out of sight and still have a clear view of the village. With day nearing its end, Moho Wat had to decide what to do. As time passed, he became more and more worried. Wind Flower was still nowhere to be seen.

The boy didn't dare leave until he was positive she wasn't somewhere right below him. If she wasn't there, how would he ever know where to look for her? He could only hope she was still here.

The Sheepeater boy had no answers to his questions. He would have to use the patience he had learned while his stump was healing. The patience he had needed to become an expert shot using his feet had taught him he could do anything if he concentrated on solving each problem. Now he hoped he could use everything he had ever learned to rescue this beautiful girl.

The day wore on. Just before dark and when it had become hard to make out peoples' faces, Moho Wat saw a woman and two men standing near a teepee. A young girl stood in the center of the three adults. The boy's heart began to beat faster. He couldn't see the girl's face, but there was the same beautiful hair, the same perfect posture, and a dress different from all the other girls' in the village.

Only a few more minutes passed, and the two warriors left. The woman took the girl by the arm and turned her toward the teepee door. Both disappeared inside the lodge and did not come back out.

That's her, Moho Wat thought. *Wind Flower is here!*

When it became too dark to see, the boy dropped to his knees under the fir branches. He smoothed out the needles that covered the ground. He broke off enough branches to make a small mattress. He unrolled his blanket. With his bow and arrows at his side, he lay down for the night.

As Moho Wat enjoyed another strip of dried meat and a handful of berries, he began to think about all that had happened in only one day. He felt lonely for his family. If only his father were with him, things would be so much better. He wondered what his family was doing and what they were thinking about their son.

Moho Wat would not sleep much this night. He had too much to think about. He also kept listening for any approaching danger. He was sure the people didn't know he was there. Still, he knew a wild animal could come by any time. He had to be ready for anything. Most of the boy's thoughts were on the dangerous rescue mission. Right now he had no idea of where or how it could be done. He would have to be like a hunter. First, he must not let the enemy discover him. Next, he would have to get close enough to Wind Flower to get her to escape with him. Finally, he would have to make the long journey home without being recaptured.

Moho Wat knew he would have to study the village and then make a plan that could work. He would just have to find the best way to do it all, contact Wind Flower, make the escape, and travel home safely. All these problems kept Moho Wat wide awake most of the night.

The next morning, even before there was much daylight, Moho Wat was watching the women leave their teepees, uncover the hot coals of their fires, and fan them into flames. The village was still very quiet. The boy kept his eyes glued to one teepee, the one he was sure Wind Flower was in. His wait was short. The woman and three children came out one by one. Two of the children were very small.

The third one, a girl, had her back to Moho Wat. When the girl turned to put wood on the fire there was that same beautiful face he had first seen on the second morning at the medicine wheel. The boy was so excited he could hardly stand still. She was right there. She hadn't been taken farther away. Now he had a chance.

As Moho Wat watched, more and more people began to move about the village. He became troubled when he saw the women begin to pack their things and take down their teepees. *No! They're going to move! Where? Where will they go?* All the boy could do was stay hidden and watch. He did start to look for a safe way to follow the enemy. He made up his mind to follow them wherever they went, no matter how far.

Moho Wat was amazed by how fast the valley people packed and started to leave. They would leave a trail easy to follow. The boy knew he would have to stay as close to his enemy as possible to make sure Wind Flower was still with them. He knew he would run the risk of being discovered. He was ready to take the chance if it meant rescuing Wind Flower. The boy didn't know it, but the next few days would be filled with unbelievable experiences that would challenge him in ways he could never dream were possible.

8

Final Plans

The first part of Moho Wat's movements were easy. He could stay hidden by trees and bushes and still have a good view of the long line of people and horses. They were following the river north. The easy part ended soon. The villagers slowly disappeared into the trees. At the same time he came to a steep open hillside. Moho Wat was stopped by the hazardous barrier.

The boy's only safe route was straight up the ridge. High above he could see the steepness decrease. Best of all there were more trees to walk in. He would have to follow the treeline up at a very steep angle. No time could be wasted. Soon the valley people would be far ahead of him.

Moho Wat started his climb at top speed. In only a few minutes his heart was throbbing in his chest. He was gasping for each breath. Sweat poured from his body. On and on the boy scrambled up the steep rise. With each passing minute his pace slowed a little. Finally, he had to stop long enough to steady his breathing. Moho Wat glanced up. He still had a long haul before he could safely turn north again.

Higher and higher the boy struggled on, using every ounce of strength he had. At last his efforts were rewarded. Moho Wat could finally turn north again. The angle was more gentle and had trees to hide him from view. It felt wonderful to walk along on an easier angle. His breathing returned to normal. A cool July breeze crossed the high ridge. No breeze had ever seemed so welcome to the sweating boy.

Moho Wat had plenty to worry about now that the villagers were completely out of sight. The more he worried the faster he began moving north. A sense of near panic began to creep into his mind. *Where are they? How can I find them from up here? Is Wind Flower still with them? I have to do something, but what? I can't let them get away. What should I do?*

Before Moho Wat panicked completely, his luck suddenly changed. The ridge he was following abruptly ended at a rocky ledge. Below the ledge a wall of sheer rock dropped straight down to the river. The boy could not walk onto the ledge. He could be seen easily by anyone with a view of the rock cliff. So he dropped to his knees and crawled toward the edge of the precipice. Six feet from the edge he lay flat on his stomach and carefully squirmed to the edge.

Right below Moho Wat's eyes was an amazing sight. Just past the cliff the river made a sharp turn and flowed due west. On the boy's side of the river a huge meadow stretched for a half a mile along the gentle riverbank. Moho Wat was astonished to see almost one hundred teepees neatly arranged over at least two-thirds of the wide meadow. The boy was shocked by the numbers of teepees and people he could see from his high perch.

After only a few minutes of taking in this dramatic scene, Moho Wat caught sight of a rider coming out of the trees on the other side of the river. Rider after rider followed. Next came the women and children. As the minutes passed, the boy became convinced that these were the people he had been following. They were headed for this meeting all along. His route had been perfect. He hadn't wasted a single step.

Moho Wat watched the whole process unfold below him as he lay flat on his stomach at the very edge of the cliff. The kidnappers forded the river through a wide shallow place. They moved up the riverbank where they were greeted warmly by the people already camped in the meadow. Soon they moved to the north end of the meadow and began setting up their teepees. As they did, Moho Wat was already planning his next move.

Moho Wat focused on a steep bluff on the other side of the river opposite the north end of the meadow. Below this sixty-foot-high bluff the river was still eroding the sand and gravel away. From the top of that bluff, the boy knew, he could see everyone at the north end of the village up close. Wind Flower would be there. He knew getting to the bluff would be dangerous, but he had a plan that would make it impossible to see him from the village. The more he studied the village the more he was sure a plan for the rescue and escape could work.

His first step in a dangerous plan was to retreat the way he had come. He would find a place to drop down to the river, cross it, circle through the trees far from the river, and come out at the bluff he had studied so carefully. He would have to find a well-hidden campsite and build a blind on the edge of the bluff that would hide him from view. From his hideout he would study every detail of the enemy village. He would observe every movement of the people. He would know where they came to the river for water, where the women and children gathered firewood, where the horses were pastured, and where the men spent their time. As a hunter knows the habits and behavior of the animals he stalks, so would Moho Wat know everything he could about his enemies. The goal of Moho Wat's hunt this time would be to save this special girl from a life of slavery.

The boy began to think about his plan and what could happen in the next days. He had a vision of making a daring rescue and a safe return of the beautiful Wind Flower to her parents. He wanted to prove that he was as good as any boy with two hands. Moho Wat longed for his mission to come true. He was ready to risk his life to make that happen.

It was time for action. The boy crawled back from the cliff and dashed into the trees. He found a safe route down the steep ridge to the river. He made the river crossing quickly. He enjoyed a long drink of cool water, which revived him instantly. All his sweating had dehydrated his body, making him feel weak and unsteady. Now his vigor returned.

On his trip through the trees to the bluff, Moho Wat crossed the trail made by the enemy villagers. His eye caught sight of something to his right on the ground. When he walked over to it, he saw it was a hide sack. It was empty. He snatched it up and sprinted into the trees. He tucked the sack under his belt and continued on.

Atop the bluff Moho Wat again squirmed on his stomach to the edge. At first sight of the village he stopped. His chin rested on the ground. The enormous village lay just below him. He was so close he could see people's faces at this end of the meadow. He was in a very dangerous place. One mistake this close and he would be discovered. Still, he didn't want to leave until he saw Wind Flower. He knew her kidnappers had set up their lodges at this end of the meadow.

Moho Wat didn't have long to wait. There she was. Wind Flower was forced to help two women erect a teepee. It was back only eighty feet from the river's edge. Only one other teepee was closer to the boy. As soon as the boy saw Wind Flower he squirmed back from the edge. He quickly came to his feet and disappeared into the aspen trees. Now came the search for a safe hiding place and camp.

Moho Wat zigzagged back and forth for two hundred yards without finding a single safe place to hide. He needed a place where no one was likely to come by and accidentally discover him. He needed a place where he would be able to see an enemy coming before they could see him. While wandering through the trees, he wondered if he would ever find such a place. He had to start soon with a plan for a daring rescue. A perfect hiding place was a must.

Just when the boy began to think he would never find the right hideout, he came to the edge of the trees and stood looking up at a rocky slope. Loose slide rock covered the lower part of the slope for a hundred feet upward. Above the loose rock lay a large boulder field. Somewhere among those gigantic boulders would be a place Moho Wat could crawl into and hide. He was sure of it.

Slowly and cautiously the boy climbed up the loose slide rock. Each step had to be made ever so carefully. Too much rock sliding would create lots of noise. It seemed to take forever to reach the boulders. At the first boulder Moho Wat stopped. Already he could see two places to climb down between boulders and be completely hidden. Before picking a place the boy let his eyes scan the boulder field in every direction. Not too far to his right he noticed a dark shadowy area. It was only a little above him. He decided it was worth checking.

In minutes Moho Wat found himself at the edge of a large opening in the boulders. He quickly took one of his many looks around to see if anyone might be watching him. After examining the large opening more closely the boy could hardly believe what he had found. The opening led into a large room-sized space. He lowered himself down onto the rocky floor. Moho Wat strained his eyes to see his sur-

roundings. Slowly his eyes adjusted to the low light. He realized he had discovered a cave under the boulder field.

Moho Wat picked his way through the darkness to the back wall of the cave. The light coming in through the opening helped him see the cavern much better. The smells told him that bears must have used the cave as their winter den over many seasons of hibernation. There was a cold damp feeling all about the boy, but here was the perfect hiding place.

Moho Wat was so excited by his fortunate discovery that a smile crossed his face. He hadn't smiled for a long time. He tingled all over with happiness at his good luck. As he started to move from the back wall toward the entrance, he suddenly came to a stop. He felt a breeze touch his back. *Where could the air be coming from?* the startled boy wondered. *How could wind blow beneath the earth?*

Moho Wat spun around and let the breeze hit his face. Keeping the air on his face he moved toward

the source of the moving air. He stumbled over a
rock and nearly fell. His curiosity had caused him
to move too quickly. He had to slow down and be
sure of every step in the darkness.

When Moho Wat reached the back wall, his hand
found a narrow opening in the rock. The air was
pouring through this wide crack. The boy was able
to turn sideways and just barely squeeze into the
crevice. In only five short slides of his feet he was
stopped. Here at the end of the narrow space he felt
the air coming down from above his head. Moho
Wat looked up and saw some light. With his hand
the boy reached above his head. Moving his hand
over the wall he came to a good handhold. Next his
left foot touched a toehold, and he was raising himself toward the source of the light and air.

The higher Moho Wat climbed the more light
there was to help him find footholds and hand-
holds. The boy's excitement grew by the second.
He realized he was coming to a second opening in
the cave. What good fortune! He had found a hiding
place that even had a hidden escape route. Up he

climbed, emerging into the open from the narrow shaft. He could see the main entrance about thirty feet below him.

In no time Moho Wat set up his camp in the cave's main room. That night in pitch darkness the boy returned to the bluff. He carried a dead bush to the edge of the bluff. It was plenty large enough for him to crawl under and be completely hidden but still have a perfect view of the enemy village. Now he was ready to make his final plans for the rescue and escape.

Back in the cave Moho Wat rolled and tossed in his blanket. Sleep would not come. His mind poured over possible plans for the dangerous rescue of Wind Flower. Somehow he had to contact the girl and let her know he was there to help her. He kept thinking about how large the village was. It was the size of the village that would help him most. He knew he might be able to walk right into the village as though he were just one of the boys who belonged there. He would use the large deerskin sack he had found to make a breechcloth that looked like the ones the rest of the boys in the village wore. He would find a way to hide his stump. His disguise would let him walk right up to Wind Flower without making anyone suspicious. This idea made Moho Wat quiver with excitement. If he was a good actor, his daring plan just might work.

The restless night ended, and Moho Wat now lay hidden under his bush at the edge of the bluff. As he watched the people below, he added the details to his plan. Step one would be his bold walk into the village carrying a load of firewood. He had seen women and children take extra loads of firewood to the three largest teepees near the center of the village. Moho Wat knew these teepees must belong to the chiefs and spiritual leaders of the people.

The second step in the plan would be to walk up to Wind Flower, stop, and show her his stump. Next he would get her to follow him through the village to the teepees of the chiefs. On the way he would tell her his plans for escape.

Moho Wat could easily see that early morning was the best time to enter the village. Only a few women were out early. No one paid any attention to others moving about that early. They were all too busy with their own work to bother to look at anyone else.

The next morning he would be ready to risk his life to save Wind Flower. He was sure the Above One had protected him so far. Now he was ready for his daring mission. The next day would tell who had the most powerful medicine, a one-handed Sheepeater boy or the powerful enemy who had him outnumbered four hundred to one.

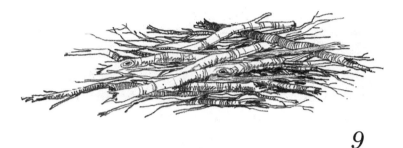

9

A Desperate Move

After a restless night in the damp cave, Moho Wat crawled out onto the boulders. There was only a slight hint of daylight in the eastern sky. The boy made his way to the river and across to the forest next to the meadow. He quickly gathered a bundle of firewood. At the edge of the trees he stopped and anxiously looked out at Wind Flower's teepee. Not a soul was stirring. He was glad. Now he could pick the very best time to make his risky move into the enemy village. He felt strangely calm as he waited and watched.

The first woman out of her teepee came from the one right next to Wind Flower's. Moho Wat's heart beat faster. The enemy woman seemed so close. Only a few minutes later a woman came out of Wind Flower's teepee. Then there she was. The girl was right behind the woman. The woman pointed at the fire, said something to Wind Flower, and went back inside.

Without wasting a second, Moho Wat walked from the trees with his firewood. He headed straight for Wind Flower. She was uncovering the coals of the fire and adding twigs to the flames already leaping skyward.

As the boy passed the first teepee he was startled by a woman walking toward him from the left. It was too late. She would pass within three feet of the intruder. Would she realize he was a Sheepeater? Would she sound the alarm? Moho Wat could do nothing but try to act normally.

The boy kept telling himself, *Keep going! Don't stop! The Above One walks with me! Keep going! Keep going!*

Moho Wat held his breath as the woman passed so closely. She never even looked at him. Her mind was on all the busy tasks she faced before the sun touched her teepee.

The boy walked on straight for Wind Flower. She was paying no attention to him. Moho Wat took a deep breath and walked right up to the girl. He stopped behind her and whispered her name. The startled girl turned around. Moho Wat pulled his stump from beneath the firewood so she could see it. When he did, part of his wood dropped on the ground.

Wind Flower's face was covered with shock and surprise. She almost cried out but held in her feelings. Moho Wat couldn't pick up the wood without putting down his whole load. Before he could kneel down, Wind Flower was already picking up the wood. The boy bent down to whisper to the shaken girl.

"I am Sheepeater. Walk with me to the big teepees," Moho Wat whispered as softly as possible.

Immediately he began walking away before anyone became suspicious. Wind Flower came up
alongside. Whenever they were far enough from
people and teepees Moho Wat told Wind Flower
about the plans for escape. The same time the next
morning he would come again with more firewood.
Again Wind Flower could follow him to the chief's
teepees. This time he would drop his wood, and
both of them would continue walking. They would
walk right through the horses, cross the river,
scramble over the boulder field and be gone before
anyone realized what had happened.

The walk to the chiefs' teepees seemed to take a
long time. More women were out and fanning their
fires to flame. None of them paid the least attention
to the boy and girl.

It's working, thought Moho Wat.

The boy felt relieved because it all seemed so
easy. But his good luck seemed to end when a huge
man came out of one of the large teepees right in
front of him. The enemy man was looking right at
him. Moho Wat quickly looked down. He strained to

watch the man's movements without looking directly at the man.

"Keep walking," the boy said to himself. *"Act naturally."*

A feeling of terror poured through the boy's mind. He broke out in a cold sweat. *What would happen if he were discovered? What would they do to him? What would they do to Wind Flower?* Moho Wat walked to the woodpile and dropped his wood. He quickly pulled a food sack from his waist and covered his stump. Wind Flower dropped her wood and both turned to walk back.

As Moho Wat made his turn around, he saw the man sitting on a mat. The man's legs were crossed, and he sat facing the rising sun. The boy took a deep breath and felt relieved once more. Even this man was not the least bit suspicious of him.

Moho Wat was still shaking from his fear of discovery as he headed for Wind Flower's teepee. The girl trailed a short distance behind. The boy walked right past the girl's teepee and headed for the trees as though he was on his way for more wood. At the edge of the forest he turned to look back at Wind Flower. Both knew that the next morning their try for freedom could result in death.

The boy's glance back at the girl would be a picture he would hold in his mind for a lifetime. The sun was just peeking over the ridge. Wind Flower's silky black hair glowed in the sun's rays. She looked so small in this huge village. Moho Wat suddenly wondered if they had a chance of making it. He wondered if they should even try. He didn't want any harm to come to this special girl.

Wind Flower's own words convinced him they must try. "I want to go home. I will be ready."

Moho Wat knew the girl meant what she said that morning. In her beautiful voice she spoke firmly with no hint of fear in her words.

The boy disappeared into the trees. Far from the village he made his river crossing safely. He spent that whole day exploring their escape route. His climb over the boulders above the cave led to a grass covered ridge that ran southwest. The ridge gradually dropped into a wide valley. Far to the west

Moho Wat could see snowcapped mountains. He knew he was looking at his goal. The valley would be dangerous. The mountains would mean safety. He knew how to travel in mountains where no enemy could follow. Up there the boy could vanish into places where no enemy would think to look.

That day seemed to drag on and on. Moho Wat could not sit still. He wondered if darkness would ever come. He didn't dare go far from his cave to hunt or gather food. He could still be found and captured. This was no time to take foolish chances. Food was a problem. He was down to three strips of dried meat and a half-handful of berries. He would have to solve his food problem after they were safely away from the enemy.

The day finally ended. The night seemed even longer. Moho Wat lay in his blanket thinking over every detail of the escape plan. He pictured every move in his mind. He could see it all happen in his mental picture of each scene. There was no way of knowing his plan would fall apart in the first ten minutes.

It was still pitch dark when Moho Wat crouched in the trees next to a bundle of firewood. The boy hid his bow and quiver of arrows inside his pile of firewood. He was ready. His eyes were fastened on Wind Flower's teepee. When she fanned her fire to flame, it would be the signal to go for it. The boy's heart pounded with anticipation. He waited motionless at the edge of the meadow.

There she was! Wind Flower had crawled from her teepee, stretched her arms, and walked to the fire. The woman in the teepee shouted at the girl but did not come out. Her words were strange sounding. Moho Wat wondered at their meaning.

In no time flames leaped from Wind Flower's fire. Moho Wat lifted his wood and walked from the trees. The escape had begun. The boy repeated his steps of the morning before. He dropped part of his wood near Wind Flower. She picked it up and used it to cover a bundle she held in her hands.

It started as an exact repeat of their trip the day before. No one paid any attention to them. Very few people were out and about their work. The timing seemed perfect. Moho Wat and Wind Flower did not see the woman come from the girl's teepee to check on her. The suspicious woman began following the two children.

Moho Wat dropped his wood on the chief's woodpile and walked on toward the horse pasture. When Wind Flower did the same, the woman began walking faster. Wind Flower realized the woman was coming. The girl quickened her pace a little. The boy had already reached the horses. He secured his quiver of arrows to his shoulder and clutched his precious bow in his right hand.

When Wind Flower reached the pasture, the woman screamed for her to come back. The pretending was over. The woman would see her bundle. In a burst of energy Wind Flower broke into a run. Startled horses galloped away. The woman screamed again. Two young warriors bolted from their teepee nearby and sprinted to the woman's side. She told them to catch the two children, grab them, and drag them back to the village.

Wind Flower had caught up with Moho Wat, and

both were in a run for their lives. The two young warriors crossed the horse pasture with long swift strides. To them this was a game. They could easily outrun children. They were closing the gap easily. It would be all over soon.

The terrified children could hear the warriors' shouts and laughter. They would be caught at the river's edge. The river was just below a small rise in front of the children. Moho Wat thought about surrender. He would say it was his fault. He would say he made the girl go with him. He would tell any lie to save Wind Flower from punishment.

Before Moho Wat could stop and surrender, everything changed. He had come over the rise next to the river. Warm moist air had been held down in the river bottom by cooler air above. The mild moist air condensed over the cold water forming a dense blanket of fog. The boy paused to let Wind Flower catch up. He whispered to her.

"The fog! It will hide us! Stay close together!"

Before the two warriors reached the top of the rise, the children had been swallowed by the dense fog. Visibility was only ten feet. Quickly the warriors split up to try to cut off the escapees.

The children ran side by side to the river's edge. Both slid down the bank and into the water. They sank into a deep pool and dog paddled to keep their heads above the surface. Silently they made their way to shallower water near the middle of the river. They stayed in knee-deep water and followed the current downstream. Moho Wat listened for any sound that would tell him the location of his enemy. He could hear nothing except the rippling water. The fog was so thick he couldn't see either bank. That meant the warriors couldn't find them without coming right into the river.

The children dared not whisper. Sound could carry to the enemy. The boy and girl used hand signals to talk to each other. They did not know that one of the warriors was on his way to the village to get help. Soon there would be a dozen warriors on each side of the river conducting the search.

Moho Wat would take no chances. Speed was important. Movement downstream went well. Luckily the boy had studied the river well. He knew exactly how far to go to reach the end of the bluff. Beyond the bluff was the way out of the river and the route to the cave.

Wind Flower and Moho Wat left the cold water and climbed the bank. Instantly the fog thinned. The boy and girl sprinted out of the fog and into the trees. They made a dash for the slide rock and the safety of the cave.

The cave was a welcome sight. The fog had saved them from capture, and now the cave would hide them until they could move on to safety. Moho Wat knew they were not free yet. He decided to keep a close lookout for more trouble. He didn't realize it, but that trouble was already on its way.

10

Baffled Warriors

Moho Wat told Wind Flower he would keep a lookout for danger. He showed her the crevice that led to the second opening. He told her to practice climbing to the secret opening. If they were discovered, that would be their only escape route. Wind Flower said nothing as she stood shivering in the cold dark cave. Now she would prepare herself for whatever might happen next.

Moho Wat felt good as he watched the treeline below. A long time had passed with no one in sight. Wind Flower climbed up next to the boy with her hand extended. She handed Moho Wat some cakes made of ground roots, berries, and meat fat. The boy smiled. Wind Flower was smart. She had secretly made a bundle for her escape. Rolled up in her blanket she had a good supply of the one thing the boy did not have: food. Now Moho Wat was sure they would make it. They had everything they needed.

Before the boy finished his last bite of food he thought he saw something in the trees. Could it be enemy warriors? The answer came fast. The two warriors who had started the chase were coming out of the trees. They were the only ones who had not given up. Somehow they had tracked the children to the clearing below. The first warrior kept pointing to the ground. Suddenly the second warrior said something that caused both of them to stop. The second warrior was pointing to the slide rock.

"They can see where the rock slid when we climbed to the cave. They are going to find us!" whispered Moho Wat.

The boy watched for a few more seconds. The two warriors were on their way to the slide rock. In a few minutes they would find the cave. Would there be enough time to pull off the most daring plan of all? Moho Wat had one final trick that just might work. The next few minutes would tell if this trick would save them. Moho Wat and Wind Flower slid into the cave.

"They're coming! Wind Flower, we have only one chance! Climb up to the secret opening. Don't go out! Wait for me there! We still have a chance!"

Moho Wat spun around and climbed back to the main entrance. With the men just sixty feet below him, the boy stood up in plain sight. When he was sure they saw him, he instantly disappeared into the cave. He headed for the crevice, squeezed inside, and quickly climbed up to Wind Flower's side.

"The warriors are coming into the cave!" whispered Moho Wat. "Climb out and help me seal the hole!"

The two children put their shoulders against a boulder and pushed with all their might. The plan

was to roll the boulder over the secret entrance blocking it forever. This would shut off the airflow and the light. The warriors would never find the escape route.

At first the boulder would not budge. Both children flexed their legs one final time. They pushed with all their might. Inch by inch the boulder moved. It happened fast. The boulder suddenly dropped over the opening. Moho Wat almost fell over with it. Wind Flower needed her hands to prevent a fall. The opening was sealed.

The warriors found their way into the cave and began their search. It was pitch dark in the cave. No breeze could be detected. No escape route could be found. The secret opening was no more. The warriors were sure the children were hidden in the cave somewhere. They knew all they needed was light, and the capture would be made.

The two warriors emerged from the cave. They said a few words, and one man left for their village. The warrior staying behind would guard the entrance. The warrior going to the village would return with hot coals from a fire. They planned to start a fire in the cave and use torches to search every possible hiding place and find the children.

Moho Wat's plan was working perfectly. He and Wind Flower crouched down until the warrior leaving was out of sight. As soon as the man was gone, the boy whispered to Wind Flower.

"Let's go! Keep low! Hurry, but don't fall!"

The two children scrambled up through the boulders, crouching as low as possible. They moved fast but were careful not to fall. An injury now would be disastrous. Moho Wat reached the top of the ridge with Wind Flower right on his heels. The children paused to catch their breath. Moho Wat tightened his bow and quiver of arrows to his shoulder. The two children sprinted down the grassy ridge to the trees below.

Moho Wat ran on glancing back often to see if the warriors were coming. There was no living thing in sight. The boy was sure his plan had worked. Back at the scene of the escape a warrior stood guarding an empty cave. It would be a long time before the baffled men discovered their mistake.

Every minute was precious. The children did not dare to stop. Every step counted. Sooner or later the warriors would resume their search for the escapees. With horses they could cover ground fast. Moho Wat knew they were still in great danger.

The day before, from the grassy ridge, Moho Wat had picked a route across the valley. He had the safest route memorized. Today that route is right along the Wyoming-Montana border passing a small town called Frannie, Wyoming. From there the route would cross the Clark's Fork of the Yellowstone River and climb into the mountains leading to the Yellowstone Plateau.

On and on the two Sheepeater children ran. Running through trees and bushes whenever possible meant jumping over logs, rocks, and roots without falling. The morning was almost gone when finally the breathless children stopped for a fifteen-minute rest. They had averaged almost six miles per hour for over three hours. Both were exhausted. The stop was made in bushes near a small creek. The water was delicious and badly needed.

Wind Flower sat quietly with her knees propped up and her head on her arms. When her head came up, she said her first words to the boy who helped her make the daring escape.

"The valley people captured me when I went for water. They made signs to me. I would be given to a chief in a far-off village to be his wife. I would be killed if I tried to escape."

Moho Wat listened to the beautiful voice. He knew he had done the right thing. He decided in his heart that even if he didn't have a chance of ever seeing Wind Flower again, he would have done a good thing.

The boy asked Wind Flower to tell him where her family would be. When she described her home valley, Moho Wat told her he did not know the place. He asked the girl to stop at the next high place and show him a mountain peak near her home. They would use it for a guide.

One final drink from the stream, and the run began again. After less than thirty minutes, Wind Flower signaled for a stop. She pointed to a western peak now called Pilot Peak.

Moho Wat smiled and blurted out, "We will make it!"

The children continued their frantic run. At every open area they stopped to look for danger. When they were sure no one was in sight, they dashed across the opening to the safety of the nearest bushes or trees. At one of these open spaces Moho Wat was ready to run for the other side. Wind Flower grabbed his arm and held him back. The girl pointed to the grass near the trees on the side farthest from them. There in the deep grass lay twin deer fawns. Their color hid them well. Their mother had left them there while she fed nearby, hidden by the bushes she nibbled on.

As soon as Moho Wat saw the fawns, Wind Flower gasped and pointed at the trees next to the fawns. Three wolves were stalking the unsuspecting fawns. The wolves' stomachs nearly scraped the ground as they slowly moved closer and closer.

One second everything was quiet and peaceful. The next second the crafty wolves were airborne and pounced on the shocked fawns. One tiny animal was able to leap to its feet. The other one didn't have a chance. Two wolves had it pinned to the ground. The mother deer sprang from the trees. Her terror-stricken fawn bounded to her side. The mother saw it was too late for her other baby. She turned and led her remaining fawn away to safety.

In a matter of seconds the wolves made their kill. One of the killers raised its head and let out a short howl. The third wolf turned back to the kill site. Moho Wat broke from the trees, his bow and an arrow in his right hand. The boy picked his spot and dropped to his back. The startled wolves were confused just long enough for the boy to draw his arrow back. His feet steadied his bow. He sighted along the arrow and sent it flying to its mark. The arrow slammed into the chest of the largest wolf and entered its heart. Death was instant. The other two wolves yelped and loped off into the trees.

Without a word Moho Wat jumped up and ran to the dead fawn. He lifted it onto his shoulder with his handless arm. The boy angled into the trees away from the wolves. He dropped the carcass and pulled a long sharp piece of obsidian from his food sack. It was better than any knife. Wind Flower held the fawn's body while Moho Wat cut away all the best meat. The girl opened her blanket still wet from the swim in the river. She laid it out flat. Both food bags were filled with fresh meat and laid on the blanket. The children chewed on delicious chunks of warm meat. The energy it gave them would be badly needed for the strenuous trip home.

The children decided to carry the food bags in their hands so their blankets could be draped over their shoulders to dry. They would need them for warmth during the coming night.

Never in her life had Wind Flower seen anything like what she had just witnessed. Moho Wat had moved so fast. When the girl saw him drop on his back, she thought something was wrong. Then came the bow to the boy's feet, the arrow pulled back, and the fatal shot hitting the mark dead center. Wind Flower knew she had been rescued by a very special boy. When their escape seemed to be failing, there was the fog bank. At the cave a warrior was fooled into guarding an empty hideout. Now their sacks were full of fresh meat. This boy with only one hand seemed to be able to do things even grown men would have a hard time doing. Now Wind Flower knew they had a good chance of making it all the way home. She didn't know that soon the boy's life would be in her hands to save or lose.

11

A Painful Rescue

With blankets draped over their shoulders to dry, the boy and girl continued their journey west. Whenever possible they walked on rocks and logs where they would leave no tracks. At every stream they waded in shallow water and left no tracks. Wind Flower was the first to notice dark clouds moving over the western mountains. There were only a few hours of daylight left. Moho Wat knew a shelter would have to be found soon. As the boy walked along, his eyes searched everywhere for shelter. Now thunder could be heard in the distance. If their blankets were soaked again, they would be faced with a miserable night.

When the thunder grew louder and louder, the sky ahead was lit by flash after flash of dramatic lightning. Moho Wat and Wind Flower quickened their pace. Now they stayed in the open to see better and move faster.

It all happened so suddenly the children had no chance to run. Thunder and wind had muffled the sound of the approaching horses. When Moho Wat and Wind Flower were in the open, five warriors on horseback came galloping toward them.

Moho Wat looked in every direction. There was no place to run or hide. It was useless. They were caught. The boy's heart sank. He felt helpless and defeated. Everything had gone so well, and now it was over. The boy glanced at Wind Flower. The girl managed a slight smile. She seemed to be saying it was all fine. He had done his best.

Moho Wat felt badly as he looked at the beautiful girl. Her eyes seemed more spectacular than ever. The boy stepped in front of Wind Flower as if to protect her from the approaching riders. He was ready with his story. He would take all the blame.

The warriors pulled their horses to a stop not six feet from the boy. Moho Wat noticed they were dressed differently from the people in the enemy village where Wind Flower was held prisoner. Who were these men? What would they do to two children?

Moho Wat was startled to hear the warrior speak the Shoshoni language perfectly. Only a few of the words were said differently from what he was used to hearing. The questions came fast.

"Who are you? What are you doing here? Where do you come from?"

Moho Wat decided to answer every question truthfully. He told the whole story of Wind Flower's capture, their escape, and their hope of returning home. The warrior asked him to tell the exact location of the enemy village. He wanted to know how many teepees there were and how many warriors.

Between claps of thunder Moho Wat gave every answer. As the boy talked, he began to relax. He realized these warriors were friendly. They were Shoshoni valley people. The kidnappers were their enemy, too.

It all ended as fast as it had started. Lightning struck a tree only one hundred yards away. The thunder was deafening. The horses reared and pranced. In an instant the riders were gone. Wind Flower looked at Moho Wat and smiled. Rain sprinkled on her beautiful face and hair. The two children ran for cover. They were lucky to find a wall of sandstone rock that had been carved out by an ancient river. There was an overhang giving them just enough room to stand clear of the rain that poured down.

Moho Wat and Wind Flower stood shoulder to shoulder against the rock wall. This would not be a good place to spend the night. Water was already running over their feet. Darkness was closing in fast. Maybe they would be forced to stand here all night. At least they were still free. The two children talked about their scare. They wondered what would happen to the Shoshoni riders.

As fast as the downpour began, it stopped. Moho Wat walked away from the overhang. He saw that the fifty-foot-high wall ran along for a quarter of a mile. Suddenly he motioned for Wind Flower to follow him. He scrambled up the wall to a wide ledge of sandstone twenty feet above the dry riverbed. The boy had just started west on the ledge when the girl called his name. He turned to see her walking east. In only a short time Wind Flower seemed to disappear into the wall.

Moho Wat followed the girl east on the ledge. There at the very end the ancient river had carved a deep hollow in the wall. It would make a perfect shelter for the night. The space was twelve feet wide and went eight feet back into the wall. The floor was covered with sand and small stones.

The children went to work. They smoothed spaces to spread their blankets and sat down to enjoy a meal of deer meat. Moho Wat caught water as it poured off the rock wall. The boy ached all over from the long run. He knew Wind Flower must be sore and tired, too. He began to wonder what the days ahead would have in store. Suddenly his thoughts were interrupted by a violent crash of thunder. The rain once again came down in sheets. The children had found shelter just in time. The rain went on and on.

Wind Flower finished her food and quietly rolled up in her blanket. The girl was sore and exhausted but never said one word of complaint. Moho Wat thought about this amazing day. Everything that had happened seemed like a dream. Finally, he, too, rolled up in his blanket to sleep.

Even though the ground was rock hard both children slept most of the night. Crashing thunder woke them up several times. It rained off and on all night. Moho Wat had a scary nightmare. He dreamed the enemy was coming, and no matter how hard he tried he couldn't run. He saw warriors with hands of giants grab Wind Flower and drag her away. The dream seemed so real it woke him up.

After his nightmare, Moho Wat sat up for a few minutes. He could hear Wind Flower talking in her sleep. He couldn't understand her words. She seemed to be half crying and half talking. He knew she must be having a bad dream, also.

When morning came, the sky was still dark and cloudy. The cold damp air sent a chill through the children. They quickly ate more deer meat and a berry cake from Wind Flower's food bag. Moho Wat secured his bow and quiver to his shoulder. He hoisted his pack to his shoulders. The day began with a walk west on the ledge. At the end a gully led to the riverbed below.

Without the sun and with clouds covering the mountains, directions would be hard to follow. From what he had seen the day before, Moho Wat knew the dry riverbed went due west and then turned north. At the turn they would have to leave the riverbed and head straight west toward Pilot Peak.

The morning passed quickly. The children continued at a steady pace. Just past noon Moho Wat and Wind Flower stood looking down at a large river. They had reached the west side of the great basin. Below them flowed the Clark's Fork of the

Yellowstone River. Beyond this river lay the high mountains and the Yellowstone country.

The river was farther away than it looked. The weather improved a little. The clouds parted several times, giving the children a glimpse of the peaks standing as guides directing their travel.

The river crossing was easy with packs held high and dry. On the opposite shore the children climbed a steep bank. Before them lay a drainage coming down out of the mountains. This seemed like the perfect route into the mountains and safety.

Moho Wat and Wind Flower walked side by side in the trees on the south side of the small creek. The stream was higher than usual because of the rain. The higher the two hikers moved, the narrower the drainage became. Again thunder could be heard high in the mountains. Moho Wat wasn't worried. There were many giant fir and spruce trees to provide shelter. Still, a great threat was building up in the distance.

On and on the children climbed. At one rest stop they talked about finally being safe from the enemy.

No horses could travel where they were hiking. No warrior could find their tracks.

"All we have to do now is keep going," said Moho Wat. "Soon we'll be in the valley of your people."

Wind Flower did not speak. Her broad smile told Moho Wat of her great joy.

The thunder became louder and louder. Moho Wat stepped out onto a grassy slope. He felt the first raindrops hit his face. On the opposite bank of the creek a short distance away stood a dozen large fir trees. They would make the perfect shelter from the storm.

To cross the creek Moho Wat had to climb down a steep bank. The other side was just as steep. The creek had carved out a deep narrow passage through the rocky soil. Wind Flower followed the boy down the bank. The boy knew he could beat the rain if he hurried.

When he was halfway down the bank a sudden roar filled the air. Things happened so fast Moho Wat had no chance to turn and climb back up the bank. He was caught in a death trap. A cloudburst high in the mountains had sent a deadly wall of water roaring down the creek. The power of the water was demolishing everything in its path.

As the wall of death reached Moho Wat, he flung himself against the rocky bank. Desperately he tried to cling to the rocks. The water hit the small boy with unbelievable force. With only one hand to hang on he didn't have a chance. A split second before being washed away to his death, the boy felt his right hand being gripped firmly. Muddy water pouring over his head blinded him. The boy gulped several mouthfuls of muddy water. The water seemed like a vicious monster trying to devour him. Suddenly his head popped out of the water. There were Wind Flower's hands wrapped like a vise around his right wrist and hand. With every ounce of the small girl's strength she pulled the boy from the clutches of the killer flood. The water slammed Moho Wat's body into the rocks. The boy dug in with his feet and held on. He was safe but badly shaken. More water could be on the way.

With Wind Flower's help Moho Wat climbed above the angry water. He saw how Wind Flower had managed to save him. She still had her legs locked around a tree like a child hanging from a playground climbing bar. She had hung upside down from the tree while grabbing his wrist to pull him from the jaws of certain death.

Moho Wat slowly raised himself to his knees and crawled up next to Wind Flower. Together they climbed out of the dangerous gully. The creek continued to rise by the second. As Moho Wat followed the girl up the bank, he was shocked to see skin torn from her legs just behind her knees. The force of the water and Moho Wat's weight had ripped the skin loose. The girl's bleeding legs would be an unforgettable sight. Wind Flower had done the impossible to save his life. The boy shook from the shock of near death.

Quickly the children found shelter in trees back the way they had just come. Wind Flower quietly spread her blanket on the bed of pine needles. Moho Wat quickly took his food bag and emptied it.

He cut it in half. The deerskin bag was soft and soaking wet. He handed the two pieces to Wind Flower to put over her torn skin to stop the bleeding. The pain was like a burning fire. Still the girl said nothing.

"You saved my life. Wind Flower, I would be dead if it weren't for you. Your strength is great. I am sorry you are hurt. I promise we will make it home. We can wait here until your legs are better. I'll do anything I can to help you."

Wind Flower smiled. Her pain was easing a little. The boy looked on helplessly. He only wished he could take her pain from her. Now he was more determined than ever to help her get home safely.

12

Slow Steps to Trouble

Both children and their blankets were soaking wet. The rain continued. The creek could be heard roaring down its narrow channel. Luckily the air was warm. Still, it would be a miserable night pinned down by pouring rain.

Moho Wat quickly snapped branches from a nearby spruce tree. He laid them crisscross fashion, making Wind Flower a mattress to keep her off the hard wet ground. She watched the boy work. She needed both her hands to hold the soft hide against her bleeding legs.

The boy finished with the branches and carefully spread Wind Flower's blanket over the top. The girl managed a slight smile and lowered herself onto the newly made bed. Moho Wat rubbed as much water from his blanket as he possibly could and gave it to Wind Flower. The boy made a mattress for himself a short distance away. Together the two children enjoyed a supper of deer meat. Wind Flower said her legs had stopped bleeding and felt better. The girl could finally lie on her side and relax.

"Thank you for making this bed. I will need only one blanket. You use yours. We both need to rest. We still have high ridges to cross."

Wind Flower's words made Moho Wat feel good. He knew this girl was not only beautiful, but she also had great courage and strength. He could still feel her hands gripping his right wrist and hand. Her powerful grip and pull against the mighty force of the wall of water had saved him from certain death. He was more sure than ever that he had done the right thing in helping Wind Flower escape the hands of her evil captors.

As darkness closed in, the night of rest and waiting began. Over and over in Moho Wat's mind he recalled each event of the last few days. Again he wondered about his father and mother. *Where could they be? What were they thinking and doing? Where was Wind Flower's family? Had they given up hope of ever seeing their daughter again? How much farther did he and Wind Flower have to go to find her home?* The more the boy thought about all these things the more he had a sure feeling that everything would end in great joy. He even could see in his mind Wind Flower dashing to her family the very second she saw them.

It was a long, long night. The boy and girl did get some sleep. As daylight came, Moho Wat sat up with his blanket still wrapped around him. He slowly rose to his feet under the low-hanging branches. He looked over to Wind Flower's bed. It was empty. The boy hurried to see if she was all right.

Moho Wat stood in shock when he saw Wind Flower. She was out in the open taking slow deliberate steps. She was stiff and sore. She was very courageous to even try to walk on her painful legs. Moho Wat didn't know what to do or what to say. His heart ached for the girl who was suffering so much after saving his life. Finally he walked over to Wind Flower and offered to help her walk.

"I am just a little stiff and a little sore," said Wind Flower. "I'll be better soon. We can still keep going."

"Wind Flower, you are injured. We can stay here until you feel better. We are safe from the enemy now. You can tell me when you are ready to walk. Then we will cross the ridges to your home. "I will be ready to go any time you feel better," said Moho Wat.

Wind Flower smiled as she slowly kept taking step by step. The rain had finally stopped. Welcome sunshine began warming the air. Moho Wat watched the girl walk stiffly into the sunlight. Her beautiful hair shone in the sun's rays. Wind Flower paused to stretch each leg and moved on through the grass and wildflowers.

As Moho Wat watched he was amazed to see the girl take each step a little more quickly and easily than the one before. The soreness and stiffness were leaving her legs. Wind Flower surprised the boy when she said she wanted to go on that very day. No matter what Moho Wat said, she insisted she was ready to continue on the way home without a rest.

After they ate some deer meat and the last of the berries from Wind Flower's bundle, the children rolled their blankets and prepared to leave. Moho Wat had been very lucky that his bow was not lost in the flash flood. But all of his arrows had been torn from his back by the vicious torrent of water. Miraculously the bow had snagged on an overhanging bush.

The climb up the creek drainage was easy at first. Wind Flower started out slowly, but after only a short distance she was moving at a normal pace. The backs of her legs right behind her knees were still raw with a little blood oozing out in a few places. Wind Flower continued without a word of complaint.

All morning the sun shone brightly. The children crossed several ridges high above timberline. By late morning they stood on a high ridge looking into a vast high mountain valley. There were no trees in sight. The bowl-shaped valley was filled with bushes, grass, wildflowers, and rocks. Wind Flower pointed to a peak in the distance on their left. Today it is called Amethyst Mountain.

"That mountain is above the valley of my people. A river goes through the valley in front of the mountain. We will be there soon," Wind Flower said excitedly.

The children picked a route through this valley which would keep them as high as possible. The north sloping ridges still had large snowbanks left over from a hard winter. The valley was much wider than it looked. Even with Wind Flower walking at normal speed the crossing of the valley took a long time.

Finally the girl asked Moho Wat if they could stop for a short rest. The boy felt badly that she had to ask for a rest. He knew he should have thought to ask her if she needed a rest stop.

During Wind Flower's rest, Moho Wat climbed a large boulder for a look at the ridge ahead. He could see the best route to follow. It ran next to a small stream created by melting snow. The route led to a rocky saddle and into the next valley. The boy returned to Wind Flower who was already standing and ready to go. Moho Wat told her about the route he had seen.

"We are very close to my valley now. I have not been this way before, but I know my valley is just ahead. I am ready," Wind Flower assured the boy.

The children set off once again. Wind Flower was a little stiff again but soon walked at a normal pace. Soon the children were moving up the ridge toward the high saddle. They walked next to a long snow-bank. They could hear water running under the snow. The melted water had created a natural tunnel beneath the deep snow. Large boulders lined both sides of the drainage. The children had to pick their way carefully through the boulders next to the snowbank.

Moho Wat had just started around a gigantic boulder when he suddenly stopped. Wind Flower nearly bumped into him. The boy thought he heard something. The sound came from the other side of the boulder he was standing next to. Instantly a great growl broke the silence. In seconds a massive sow grizzly bear came charging around the boulder. Less than thirty feet from Moho Wat the great bear rose up on her hind legs and pawed the air.

The boy grabbed Wind Flower by the hand. "Jump onto the snow!" shouted Moho Wat.

In seconds the children had scrambled up on the snowbank and were sliding down the steep snowy slope at unbelievable speed. The six-hundred-pound grizzly ran next to the snowbank on course to meet the children at the end of their slide.

Down and down plummeted the horrified children. At their speed the boy and girl would go over the end of the snow and smash into the rocks

below. As the children neared the lip of the long snowbank, they frantically dug their fingertips into the snow to slow their speed. Moho Wat used his stump, jamming it into the snow that had been softened by the warm sun.

"Stay with me!" shouted Moho Wat.

As the two children slid over the lip of snow, Moho Wat locked his arm under Wind Flower's arm. The two children landed together in the water five feet below them. Instantly they were scrambling into the snowy tunnel. The angry bear bounded into the water and stuck its head into the tunnel. The children were already in the narrowest part of the tunnel. Their backs were rubbing against the ceiling of the snowy cavern. Above the sound of the running water, the echo of the mother bear's growls sent chills through the children.

The bear stood at the tunnel's entrance for only two minutes. The children had escaped this sow grizzly who thought they had come to harm her six-month-old cub. Moho Wat realized they had lost something else in the flash flood. Shoshoni elders tell of a special plant they used to ward off grizzly attacks. The boy had such a plant tied around his neck. It had been torn away by the force of the water. Wind Flower had lost her protective plant during her captivity.

The children huddled in their cold, dark shelter. The icy water made their feet cold and numb. Finally Moho Wat crawled back to the entrance and carefully peered out. He was relieved to see the mother grizzly and her cub side by side heading down into the valley.

Quickly the children emerged from their icy hideaway and resumed their climb through the boulders to the ridge crest. At the ridge top Wind Flower let out a cry of joy. "This is the valley of my people!"

It was late afternoon. There would not be enough daylight to make it to Wind Flower's wicki-up. Another half day of travel lay ahead. The children descended the steep ridge and reached the dense forest right at dark. They found the shelter of a great fir tree for the night. Neither of them could sleep. They sat wide awake all night talking excitedly about all that had happened and about the day ahead.

Moho Wat learned all about Wind Flower and her family. He told her about Eagle Claw, his mother, and his father. He told about discovering the sheep's horn softening in the boiling water. He described the mountain lion's attack and what it was like to have only one hand. Never before had Moho Wat talked to anyone the way he talked to Wind Flower that night. To him it seemed like living in a dream.

At the first hint of daylight the children were on their way. This time Wind Flower took the lead. She talked about the river they were following. She knew every bend and every rapids in the Lamar River. This river is located in a secluded valley in what today is Yellowstone National Park.

In her growing excitement Wind Flower walked faster than ever. She had completely forgotten about her sore legs. Moho Wat had to work hard to keep up with the excited girl.

It was near the middle of a beautiful sunny day when Wind Flower made a right turn and scurried into the dense trees. After only twenty minutes, Wind Flower let out a cry of joy. Moho Wat watched as the girl dashed into her mother's arms. The startled mother could hardly believe her eyes. Her little Wind Flower had come home. Wind Flower's little brother and sister ran from their wicki-up and into their big sister's arms. Moho Wat awkwardly stood watching as this Sheepeater family poured out their love so freely.

When everyone had calmed down, the questions started. Wind Flower's father asked about Moho Wat, and the girl blurted out the news about her rescue. Soon everyone was sitting down to listen to the whole story. It was the most unusual tale this family had ever heard.

When Wind Flower finished, her father said he had a story to tell. His story ended with great news for Moho Wat. Wind Flower's father told the boy his mother and father were staying in a wicki-up only a short distance away. Moho Wat's father had told

Wind Flower's family that somehow he knew the Above One would let the children return someday. The boy's father even said he thought his son had gone to try to rescue the girl. That afternoon it was Moho Wat's turn to run with joy in his heart to his mother and father. That day the boy would hear his father say, "My son, today you have proved that you are as good as any man. You have shown your bravery and your goodness. I am proud of my son, Moho Wat."

These words that his father had said to him after he had lost his hand would now ring in Moho Wat's heart forever. And, yes, soon Moho Wat's father and mother would speak to Wind Flower's mother and father about the marriage of these two young people when they became of age. To seal the promise of this marriage Moho Wat's father would give Wind Flower's father a beautiful sheep's horn bow. In the years ahead the amazing bows made from the sheeps' horns would be treasured by all bow hunters.

Epilogue

In their early teenage years Moho Wat and Wind Flower would marry. In their own wicki-up they would raise their own family. The sheep's horn bow would serve Moho Wat well. He would make many more bows and trade them for things his family could use. Wind Flower would tell her children the story of her capture and how their father outsmarted the enemy to rescue her.

The descendants of Moho Wat and Wind Flower would see the non-Indians come and declare their homelands to be Yellowstone National Park. All the Sheepeater people would be told to leave the new park forever. At the same time a hideous disease,

smallpox, would strike the Sheepeater people, causing their deaths. Against this vicious enemy there
would be no defense. But even today Sheepeater
wicki-ups can still be found standing as reminders
of these Indian people. They were the only known
year-round residents of the first and most famous
national park in the world. Hanging in a display
case in the Colter Bay Museum is a beautiful
sheep's horn bow, one of the few in existence. It
hangs there as a reminder of the great ingenuity of
a very special group of Indian people.